Jubilant Soul

BOOK ONE

D0103891

THE SOMEDAY LIST

A Novel

Stacy Hawkins Adams

Revell

a division of Baker Publishing Group
Grand Rapids, Michigan

© 2009 by Stacy Hawkins Adams

Published by Revell
a division of Baker Publishing Group
P.O. Box 6287, Grand Rapids, MI 49516-6287
www.revellbooks.com

Printed in the United States of America

Library of Congress Cataloging-in-Publication Data
Adams, Stacy Hawkins, 1971–
    The someday list : a novel / Stacy Hawkins Adams.
        p.   cm. — (Jubilant soul ; bk. 1)
    ISBN 978-0-8007-3266-0 (pbk.)
    1. Married women—Fiction. 2. Conduct of life—Fiction. 3. Family—Fiction.
4. Texas—Fiction. I. Title.
    PS3601.D396S67 2009
    813′.6—dc22   2008039422

To my sister, Patsy Scott,
for serving as a modern-day Lazarus,
and reminding those who know and love you
that God can, and still does, work miracles.

No, dear brothers and sisters, I have not achieved it, but I focus on this one thing: Forgetting the past and looking forward to what lies ahead.

Philippians 3:13 NLT

PROLOGUE

Rachelle fumbled with the bouquet of yellow roses and locked eyes with him. Her flowers sagged from thirst.

The simple gold band she clutched stuck to her sweaty palm. Instead of a flowing white gown, she wore the black pencil skirt and short-sleeved white silk blouse that, until today, had served as her choral ensemble uniform.

Her groom was dressed in his standard singing attire too—white collared shirt, black tie, and black slacks. He had removed the diamond earring from his left earlobe, his goatee was freshly cut, and as far as she was concerned, he had never looked finer.

Between the two of them, the worldly goods they possessed amounted to less than what Rev. Prescott likely paid to have his preaching robe cleaned.

And yet, she knew this was right. The right time, the right place, and the right man, even if she had to marry him in secret. One day they would look back on this elopement with tenderness and pride, telling their children about their union in an empty church sanctuary, not far from the university they would graduate from in six months.

He smiled at her and arched an eyebrow, questioning the delay in her response. The minister repeated himself.

"Rachelle Marie Mitchell, do you take this man to be your lawfully wedded husband?"

She smiled. Her beloved didn't have to worry about her having second thoughts—not when she felt this way.

"I do, Reverend Prescott," she said. "I do."

1

*R*achelle Mitchell Covington felt both giddy and guilty.

In twenty-four hours she would be completely alone and she couldn't wait.

No worries about temporary empty-nest syndrome—she was happy to let her parents deal with two preadolescent know-it-alls for half of the summer. And no need to feign an interest in her husband's wants, work, or even his world.

For the first time in their eleven-year marriage, she and Gabe would be away from each other for more than a week. When he informed her that he had agreed to speak at a medical conference the week before he left for a medical mission trip, she knew he expected her to complain. Rachelle had frowned for his benefit, but also bit her lip to keep from cheering.

Though it was already steamy outside this morning, the temperature inside Houston's Intercontinental Airport left her longing for her cashmere coat. Rachelle shivered and smiled when Tate and Taryn, looking like they had stepped off the pages of a *Children's Wear Digest* catalog, turned to wave one last time before passing through the security gate and approaching a waiting airline employee.

The young woman in the crisp navy and white uniform would escort them to their direct flight to Philadelphia.

The fifth and third graders had been trying to whine their way out of their annual summer visit with Rachelle's parents for two days, because they would miss their friends, feared boredom, and believed Gram would have way too many rules. Rachelle had reminded them again this morning that, despite those perceived hardships, they had no problem enjoying the regular outings, video games, and other treats they enjoyed during their stay.

When Tate and Taryn disappeared around a bend that led to Terminal A, Gabe turned toward Rachelle and motioned with his head that he was ready to go. He and Rachelle walked briskly toward the parking deck without touching or talking.

Gabe walked a stride or two ahead of her, as if he were on a mission. He tempered his gait as they neared his SUV, and he unlocked the doors with his key chain device.

"I'm not going into the office this morning since I'll be flying out early tomorrow," he said without looking toward Rachelle. "Let's grab breakfast at Olivette."

Rachelle scrambled for an excuse, but none presented itself. She hadn't mentioned that she soon would be leaving too, for a weekend trip to the West Coast. It didn't matter that he didn't know. He wasn't going to be home anyway.

"That's fine," she finally said about breakfast, although he had already steered his Mercedes in the direction of the hotel restaurant.

They rode in silence during the half-hour drive and didn't speak until the waitress asked for their order.

Rachelle sighed and responded by rote. "He'll have smoked salmon and a bagel with a side of fresh fruit."

Gabe nodded and looked up at the waitress. "She got it right."

"Salmon and bagel with a side of fruit," the waitress repeated, lodging the order in her memory.

Rachelle leveled her eyes at Gabe. "Order for me."

He peered at her over the rim of his glasses. "How would I know what to order for you?"

Rachelle didn't feel like playing along with his public politeness today. She sat back and folded her arms.

"Try."

The waitress shifted from one foot to the other and turned her gaze to a nearby bank of potted plants.

Gabe's nostrils flared and he clenched his teeth. "Just order something already."

"If you can't do it, I guess I'm not hungry," Rachelle said.

Gabe opened the leather-encased menu and glared at the offerings. Seconds later, he pushed it into the waitress's face. Startled, she grabbed it before it landed on the Oriental rug beneath the table.

"Bring her an omelet with ham, mushrooms, and cheddar cheese."

The waitress nodded and left quickly, her reddish-brown ponytail swaying with each step. Rachelle knew the young lady had to be wondering how a couple could fight over a breakfast order. If she had asked, Rachelle would have assured her this skirmish was overdue.

Since she had received Jillian's unsettling invitation three weeks ago, Rachelle's tolerance for just about everything had plummeted. With the kids away for the next month, she didn't have to contain herself. Gabe should be thankful he was leaving for a business trip tomorrow.

He laid his linen napkin across his lap and stared at her.

11

Rachelle challenged him with her eyes. She wanted him to care enough to question her, to probe why she was being defiant.

But just as she knew what to order for his meal, she knew he wouldn't take the bait. He was his usual, detached self—enveloped in skin that was a smooth, savory brown and as self-absorbed as a two-year-old whose favorite words were "no" and "mine."

In that moment, something welled up inside of her. She looked past Gabe's glasses, past the perfect white teeth, past the pool of nothingness in his eyes. She wanted to see into his soul. She wanted to know that he had an "I would die for you" kind of love inside of him. For her. Even if they had been together for what seemed like forever. Even if she didn't know how she really felt about him. If one of them could summon the emotion, maybe that would make all the difference.

He was leaving tomorrow for New York and would return home for one day before traveling to Uganda. In twenty-four hours, she'd have the entire house to herself. But right now, she realized, she needed to leave to save herself.

Right now, what mattered more than being a good wife was being good to herself. Hearing from Jillian for the first time in a long time was nudging her to stop procrastinating.

Rachelle took a sip of her coffee and rose from her seat. "Stay and enjoy your breakfast. Call a taxi when you're done. I may or may not be at home by then."

"What—"

Before he could protest, Rachelle raised her hand to stop him. Her voice trembled when she addressed him in a whisper. "Gabe, I'm tired of playing like the happy couple. Our life is strangling me. I want a real marriage and this isn't it . . . And by the way, I've always hated cheddar cheese."

She grabbed her purse from the back of her chair and strode

toward the door, heart pounding as if it would burst through her sleeveless tangerine top.

Had she really done that? Did she just walk away from her well-to-do, handsome husband and leave him stranded in a restaurant?

What would her parents say? Their friends? For the first time that she could recall, those questions wouldn't determine her actions.

Rachelle slowed her pace when she reached the restaurant's entrance and nodded farewell to the hostess. She strode through the lobby of the Houstonian Hotel and thanked the bellhop who held open the door for her. While the valet retrieved Gabe's Mercedes truck, she stood at his booth, tapping her foot and looking over her shoulder.

In the minutes since she had left the table, Gabe hadn't pursued her. Despite the fact that she had fueled this drama, she was hurt. She breathed in the humid summer air and exhaled slowly, trying to keep her composure. For once, she wished she were sweaty enough to mask the moisture on her face. The last thing she wanted to admit was that once again, she had allowed him to make her cry.

2

*R*achelle sat in the middle of her four-poster bed an hour later, staring into space. She clutched a cordless phone to her ear and listened to her younger sister's nasal drawl.

"Girl, no you didn't do that to that man," Alanna said. "How could you, when you know he's leaving for his medical conference tomorrow and then going to Africa?"

Rachelle shrugged as if her sister could see her through the phone. Alanna lived four hours away, in Dallas, but they talked at least three times a week, sometimes more if one of them had a pressing issue.

"I didn't plan it, Lanna," she said. "It just happened. I couldn't help myself. I don't think I'm really leaving him; I just want him to know how unhappy I am. I want him to put some effort into this marriage, other than just paying the bills."

"But, Rachelle," Alanna said dryly, "by tomorrow morning you would have had your space, without causing all of this drama. And believe me, paying the bills is nothing to sneeze at. What gives?"

Rachelle remained silent for what felt like an eternity while Alanna waited. She didn't want to go into details about the turmoil Jillian's news had thrown her into, and other than that, she had no explanation.

"When I find out, I'll let you know," Rachelle said. "I'm going to go pack for him and for myself. I don't think I told you—I'm going to California for the weekend. Jillian lives there now, remember?"

Alanna sniffed. "You haven't seen Jillian in years. Why fly across the country now? Don't get there and start wallowing in your memories of what coulda shoulda been. Hopefully when you come back, Gabe won't have changed the locks."

Rachelle ignored her sister's cynicism. Alanna didn't know that Jillian needed her. Plus, she had always questioned how Rachelle had landed such a good man while she—despite her "fabulosity"—still found herself catching frogs.

"Girl, you don't know how good you have it," Alanna would often tell Rachelle after relaying the details of another breakup with a boyfriend she hadn't known was married, on medication, or afraid of commitment.

Before the conversation went down that path this afternoon, Rachelle ended the call and began packing for a brief stay in San Diego. Her flight didn't leave for another two days but this would give her something to do, other than watching the clock to see what time Gabe made it home. Usually she was too busy with Tate and Taryn to notice, but with them gone, she needed to keep herself occupied.

She intended to visit California for less than forty-eight hours, but that still meant a large suitcase, because she could never decide what to wear. Rachelle tucked her digital camera and a scrapbook of childhood photos of herself and Jillian between her favorite knee-length cocktail dress and a floor-length emerald green one. She added a pair of jeans and shorts and a few casual tops, in

15

case there was some downtime with Jillian, or, more likely, the other guests. When her bag was ready, Rachelle sat it in the back of her closet.

She padded across the plush plum carpet and walked into Gabe's closet. She surveyed his collection of bags and retrieved a small suitcase from a low-level shelf.

Packing for him came as easily as ordering his meals. It took minutes to fill the designer luggage with several white shirts, ties, slacks, and the suit he needed for his medical conference. She pulled out a large hard-shell suitcase for the mission trip to Uganda.

"Might as well get all of it out of the way," she muttered.

Rachelle walked over and sat on Gabe's side of the bed. She rummaged through his nightstand for the list of recommended travel items the medical mission leader had given to the "freshmen" on the team—him, another doctor in his practice, and a surgical nurse, all of whom were first-time participants.

Three pairs of khakis—check. Five long-sleeved shirts and a few T-shirts—check. Socks, underwear—check. Sneakers—check. Insect repellent . . . the list went on and on.

She slid his supply of over-the-counter medicine and malaria pills into plastic zipper bags, tucked his first-aid kit in the suitcase's interior pouch, and made sure he had his passport.

Rachelle closed the oversized bag and placed it in a corner, near the bedroom entrance. She was preparing to organize her shoe closet when she heard Gabe climbing the winding staircase.

His slower than usual pace cued her that he was ticked off.

By the time he reached the upstairs landing and leaned against the bedroom door, her heart was racing. She looked up from her task and returned his glare.

"What's going on with you?" Gabe uttered more of a challenge than a question.

Rachelle walked over and paused in front of him, taking in his thin lips, now frozen in the straight line they always made when he was angry. She gazed at the thick eyebrows that Tate and Taryn had inherited before allowing her eyes to skim his angular face and chiseled chest and wander down to his hands—miracle hands, he called them—that were now perched at his hips in frustration.

She was average height, but having to look up to him always made her feel smaller. She moved in close enough to feel his breath on her face and inhale the intoxicating cologne she had given him for his birthday, but she still didn't answer him.

Rachelle was tempted to try again to express all that she had been feeling over the past few weeks, but thought better of it. When had he ever cared to understand her perspective about anything?

Lately, the few times she had tried to be romantic or give him extra attention had only led to more frustration. The dinners she prepared for just the two of them had grown cold while she waited for him to get home from the hospital or his office, without even a call to let her know he had been delayed. When he did come home early enough to spend time with Tate and Taryn and retire with her for the night, he'd be too weary for pillow talk about her day or the kids' activities. Before she could finish a thought, he'd be fast asleep. Why bother to broach a subject about something more meaningful, like her restlessness? Instead, she would beat him at his own game today: his questions didn't deserve her answers.

"What do you mean?" she asked and looked into his eyes. "I'm doing my 'wifely duty,' aren't I? Your bags are all packed for the conference and even for this mission trip you're so excited about." She tilted her head. "Wonder what your partners would say if they knew you could care less about those poor children in Africa, other than what they can do for your résumé."

Gabe narrowed his eyes. "Don't change the subject, Rachelle. You left me stranded downtown, at a hotel restaurant frequented by people we know. Do you know what that looked like? My picture appears in the paper for a feature on the upcoming mission trip and my wife walks out on me days later in a public place? Don't you know this could get back to the other docs and be very damaging?"

Rachelle willed herself not to cry. "I wish I knew what was going on, Gabe. All I can say is that I'm tired. I'm not happy with myself or with us, and I'm sick of pretending that everything is perfect. It takes too much work."

Gabe moved around her and turned toward the mahogany dresser, where he pulled out a pair of jeans and a T-shirt.

"Nothing is good enough for you, Rachelle—not this big house and a maid, not the new car you have to have every few years, not even your access to enough money to do whatever you want, without having to work. And let's not even talk about the two gorgeous kids. What's the problem?"

Resentment churned in her gut. "There you go again, listing *things*," Rachelle said. "Actually, I went through childbirth, so I gave you the kids, Gabe. And, if you'll recall, I never asked to be a kept woman. I'm an optometrist, remember? I enjoyed the few years I worked in my field. I became a stay-at-home mom because that was what you wanted. But I'm beginning to wonder if you've ever really given me what mattered most—you. I'm wondering if you even know what that means, or if I do."

He frowned at her and stepped into his jeans. "Where is all of this coming from? Why are you talking about optometry when you haven't practiced in almost a decade? What is wrong with you?"

Rachelle shook her head. She walked over and stood in front of him and continued as if he hadn't spoken. "I was just a 'right'

18

choice, Gabe, wasn't I? Like all the other choices you made to fit into your parents' world. Right career? Medicine. Right family? Pretty wife and kids. Right neighborhood? Tanglewood. When have you ever done something just because you decided on your own that it was important or special, without worrying about what your parents wanted or about keeping up with everyone else? Have you ever done that?"

Rachelle saw that she had hit a nerve. Gabe was speechless. He quickly recovered, though, and rolled his eyes.

"Girl, you sound like you're having a midlife crisis," he said. "You're too young—snap out of it. After this conference, I'll be gone for just about three weeks. That's enough time to get yourself together. Maybe you can get a part-time gig at that boutique you love while the kids and I are out of the house. Or find another volunteer opportunity to whet your appetite. Or maybe you and your girlfriends should go to that spa you like in Austin. Just don't do what you did this morning. Ever again."

Rachelle surprised herself when she grabbed his arm before he could walk away.

"If we're going to fix this, you have to be present, Gabe," she said. "You can't keep barking orders and disappearing."

He chuckled and shrugged out of her loose grasp. His disdain struck her like a slap in the face.

"You know what? I need some time to myself right now, so I can think clearly," she said.

Gabe gave her a quizzical look. "What does that mean?"

She didn't answer.

"You can't change the past, Rachelle," he said. "You're married to me now."

She shifted her gaze. Hadn't that always been one of their issues? Lingering shadows from her past?

19

Gabe mistook her silence as surrender and changed the subject. "I need to be at the airport in the morning by six a.m. for my flight to New York. The other docs are meeting me in front of the Delta terminal so we can check our bags all at once. And knowing Stevens, he's going to want to pray or something before we board the plane. I need you there."

She hesitated. That was the least she could do. But the good angel that usually sat on her shoulder continued to bat zero today. "How about I 'pray' for you now? I need to take care of me. I'm leaving for a while."

Stunned by her own boldness, Rachelle turned away from him before her eyes betrayed her. What was she talking about? She wasn't scheduled to fly to California until Friday—two days from now. At that moment, however, she decided not to waver. She obeyed whatever her heart told her to do these days. God forgive her if this time she were wrong.

3

*G*abe laughed and walked away. "You ain't going no-where." He folded his arms and paced the bedroom floor. "You're married to one of the top cardiac surgeons in the nation. I chose you, and now you're trying to step out? Please."

He bent over to grab his shoes and chucked them in his closet, then walked out of the bedroom. Rachelle knew where he was headed—to the third level of the house where he could unwind with his wall-length flat screen TV, his Wii, and his wet bar.

In a few hours, he would be so tipsy he might not remember this conversation. Or at the very least, he'd have an altered memory of what their argument had been about and how it had been resolved. Happened every time they had a fight.

Rachelle returned to her closet and grabbed a canvas bag to hold a few pieces of clothing and toiletries.

She plodded down the stairs and into the kitchen, where she looked around and took a deep breath. Her heart pounded so frantically she was sure Gabe could have heard it, if he cared to listen.

She opened the door leading from the kitchen to the three-car garage and put her luggage on the backseat of her silver Lexus.

She slid behind the wheel and sat there for a few minutes. Was she really doing this? Did she know what it could mean?

Years ago, she would have probably paused to pray, but she hadn't talked to God in so long that now she wouldn't know what to say. No matter what her Aunt Irene always said about him being on time, Rachelle was almost certain that rule applied only to dues-paying servants.

She brushed away those thoughts and pressed the garage door panel near the windshield of her car. She knew Gabe was blasting his music or the TV and wouldn't hear her leave. He'd go ballistic when he realized she hadn't been bluffing.

The thought made her smile. Finally, she had found a way to shake him. His cell phone rested on the charger in the kitchen. She called it instead of the home phone so Gabe would receive the message later.

"I'm going away for the night, to clear my head and take care of myself," Rachelle said on his voice mail. "Have a nice flight to New York and enjoy the conference."

She didn't say whether she would see him when he returned. In the rush of actually doing something independent of him, she wasn't sure she wanted to reassure him. Gabe needed to feel some of the conflicting emotions she had been wrestling with for a long time. She had reached her limit.

Just before sunset, Rachelle pulled in front of one of Houston's fanciest downtown hotels and ended a winding, two-hour drive across the metro area. She checked into the Magnolia with the travel bag that contained her sleepwear, a jogging suit, and her iPod.

She entered her suite and flung herself across the bed, onto her back. She stared at the patterned ceiling and shook her head. *I can't believe I'm doing this.*

She lay there for half an hour and let her thoughts wander. She should call her parents to make sure the children had arrived safely. She should check in with Gabe, but then again, why bother?

When she finally sat up to survey her quarters, Rachelle zoned in on a set of double doors that led to a well-lit bathroom the size of a large walk-in closet. Inside, she found scented candles and complimentary bubble bath awaiting her.

She filled the Jacuzzi-style tub with the lavender-scented gel and warm water. When water lapped near the edge, she peeled off her clothes and slowly slid inside. Rachelle positioned her shower cap–covered head against the tub's ledge and reviewed how she had gotten to this place, both physically and emotionally, and why she was throwing her security to the wind.

Had she really left her husband sitting in a restaurant this morning with no ride home? Was she really leaving it up to him to get himself to the airport tomorrow? Rachelle Mitchell Covington? Miss Goody Two-Shoes?

She laughed out loud. It was short and quick, tempered by a pang of regret.

Just because she could act so foolishly didn't make it right. She sat there, considering what her options would be if she stayed with Gabe and what she might face if she chose to leave. Soon, the tears came, first a trickle and then in buckets.

Why, she wasn't sure.

Maybe for Jillian. Or for herself. Or for Gabe. Or for what could have been that maybe never would be.

When she was spent, Rachelle sat up in the tub and shivered. She'd been there so long that the water had turned cool. She reached for the spigot for a fresh surge of wet warmth, but realized that what she really wanted was out of her control.

Adoration from her husband, maybe? A joint effort to reduce this gap of nothingness between them before he left the country? She wanted . . . She needed . . .

Sadly, this was the issue. She wasn't sure where the empty place deep inside of her resided. That meant she also wasn't sure how to fill it.

Could it be that this isn't about Gabe at all?

Rachelle banished that frightful thought without giving it full consideration. She rose from the tub and wrapped herself in an oversized towel. When she was dry and dressed in a peach silk nightgown and matching robe, she strolled into the sitting area of the suite and curled up on the sofa. She stared out of the fourteenth-floor wall of windows at the starry sky.

Was there really a God up there?

The notion of a loving higher power was understandably attractive for those who needed a way to connect with other people for a common cause, but if you were self-reliant, some of what most churchgoers called faith seemed like mindless devotion. That was one thing upon which she and Gabe still agreed.

Soon after they married, she had joined the church he had grown up in, and they had attended during holidays and other special occasions to make his mother happy. But since Geraldine's death several years ago, Gabe hadn't suggested that they return.

"My mother never liked the minister anyway," he had replied when she asked why they no longer went. Rachelle had secretly enjoyed the sermons and the music whenever they visited, but she knew if she insisted on attending, Gabe would run faster in the other direction.

Sundays had been filled with golf outings, brunch with friends and colleagues, and weekend getaways with other doctors and their wives. Church became an afterthought. So much so, that Rachelle had all but forgotten what was so meaningful about regularly attending services and worshiping an unseen force.

Tonight, however, she peered into the darkness and pondered whether there was something to this faith that her favorite aunt and uncle had always raved about when she visited them during her years in college. She wished she had something or someone here now, to guide her.

Do you have any answers for me, God? If you're real, can you show me?

Claps of thunder didn't rattle her ears and the sky didn't part. Rachelle sighed. That would have been too simple.

Her cell phone rang and she dashed to pick it up before the call was routed to voice mail.

"Mommy, where are you?"

Tate's high-pitched voice made her smile. "Hi, sweetheart," she said. "How was the flight?" She wiped her eyes and focused on her son's responses.

"No turbulence this time. And Gram was so happy to see us. She took us for pizza, and then we went to the park to watch the sunset."

Rachelle grinned. Tate had already forgotten the complaints he had spouted all the way to the airport this morning. Gram got an A-plus for wowing him on the first day of his stay.

"I'm glad you had such a good day, baby. Sounds like your visit is off to a great start. Behave yourself, now."

"Okay, Mommy. But why did Daddy tell me to call you on your cell phone? Where are you?"

Rachelle hesitated. "What did Daddy say?"

"He just said to call you; you had to go out and do something."

"Daddy's right, sweetie," Rachelle said softly, thankful that Gabe hadn't brought their son into this.

She asked to speak to Taryn and reminded her daughter to listen to Gram and to have a good time. "I love you, little lady."

"Love you too, Mom."

When had this eight-year-old become too grown up to call her "Mommy"? Rachelle's heart sank.

She ended the call and glanced at the digital alarm clock next to the bed. It was 9:30 in Philly and 8:30 p.m. here in Houston.

Rachelle rose from the sofa and stretched. She walked over to her bag and pulled out the outfit she planned to wear tomorrow. She slipped out of her nightgown and into the navy blue stretch pants and matching pullover top.

This has been the shortest, and as a result, the most expensive, hotel stay of my life.

Something was leading her home. Nothing had changed, really, but after hearing her babies' voices, she knew that this couldn't be all about her. She had to do right by them.

She picked up her cell phone and dialed the house.

It rang until the call was routed to voice mail. Rachelle was surprised, but surmised that Gabe was probably blasting his music or taking a shower so he'd be ready to catch his pre-dawn flight. Or maybe he was so mad that he was ignoring her call.

She plopped onto the bed and sat there, Indian style, debating her options.

If she left for home now, Gabe would be asleep by the time she arrived and not realize she was there. When he awoke to prepare for his trip, he'd see her and believe he had won—she had returned, just as a submissive, grateful wife should.

She pictured the contempt in his eyes and saw his smug smile.

Why wouldn't the wife he owned show up to do her duty and get him to the airport?

The more Rachelle thought about it, the less she wanted to go.

She wished she had some answers, some direction on what to do. She wished she could talk to someone about it—her mother, her sister, or even her friends.

But Mom wouldn't understand—she believed you got married and you stayed married, whatever it took. Alanna was too man-hungry to see straight, let alone to offer levelheaded advice. And her friends? None of those divas could hold water. If she confided in any one of them, she might as well be ready to see her woes on the front page of the *Houston Chronicle*.

Rachelle reached for her iPod and turned to the songs she had downloaded in recent weeks—Beyoncé's "Listen" and Jennifer Hudson's "I Am Changing" from the movie *Dreamgirls*.

She played them over and over as she lay across the bed with her eyes closed, dressed but unsure of what to do.

Finally, sleep won.

With heavy eyes, she pulled back the covers on the queen-sized bed and crawled underneath, fully dressed. She was too old to be this lazy, but oh well.

Rachelle reached over to the bedside nightstand to set the alarm clock and turn off the light. A blue, hardcover Bible caught her eye.

For a second, she was tempted to pick it up and open it.

You won't understand it anyway.

That unbidden voice was right. It was probably written in the King's English, and right now, she doubted she could decipher Ebonics. Sleep couldn't come fast enough.

Unless she felt differently in a few hours, she would go home and offer to drive Gabe to the airport. For now, she was going to rest.

Rachelle drifted to sleep with the image of Jillian's party invitation before her, as it had been most of the nights since it had arrived in the mail:

> I'm dying. Soon. Please join me at 6
> p.m. on July 15 at one of San Diego's
> most beautiful restaurants. We'll gather
> at George's at the Cove, in the Ocean View
> Room, to celebrate our friendship and my
> life's journey before I go to be with God. No
> gifts, please. I can't take them with me!

In her heart of hearts, Rachelle knew this message from a long-ago friend had triggered her marital and personal angst. Now she had to figure out what to do about it without causing her world to implode.

4

Who would throw a party to celebrate her death?

Only Jillian Parks. Age thirty-six. Stricken with breast cancer. Given six weeks to live.

Rachelle had marveled over that decision since receiving the invitation to this evening's gathering at one of San Diego's most elegant ocean-view restaurants. She and Jillian hadn't talked in years, but Rachelle stood here tonight, awestruck, as she watched her childhood best friend greet a roomful of friends and relatives.

Rachelle stood near a wall of windows that featured lapping waves as the backdrop. Her eyes kept pace as Jillian's husband, Patrick, pushed Jillian's wheelchair wherever she directed.

Dark circles had settled beneath her friend's amber eyes, but they still lit up when she paused to chat with guests who lingered over a generous seafood buffet or stood in somber small groups, chatting softly. Jillian was waiflike, but even cancer hadn't stolen her beauty, Rachelle decided.

Jillian hadn't lost her flair for fashion, either. Tonight she wore an ankle-length, soft gold gown that featured one strapless shoulder. The wavy, black hair Rachelle remembered had been replaced with a Pocahontas-style wig that complimented Jillian's oatmeal complexion.

Forget that they hadn't spoken in a decade. How could Rachelle not be here? She surveyed the chandeliered room of seventy-five or so people who, like her, had come to shower Jillian with love. They too seemed surprised by her festive mood.

Rachelle's eyes watered when Patrick pushed Jillian up the wheelchair ramp onto a wooden platform that had been temporarily positioned in the middle of the expansive dining room.

Everyone gathered, and Jillian smiled when she reached the center of the makeshift stage. The ocean behind her served as a natural mural.

Had she chosen to speak now, specifically because the sun was setting over the water? Rachelle wondered. The scene was simply beautiful, and fitting of such a special occasion.

Jillian picked up the microphone that had been resting on her lap and held it to her ruby red lips. She scanned the room, seeming to peer into the eyes of everyone present, including Rachelle's. Finally, she spoke.

"Thank you all for coming tonight. Some of you traveled from the opposite coast to be here with me. Some of you altered plans to be here. Some of you had to work financial miracles or request time off from work to join me, and for all of that, I'm grateful."

She extended her hand toward Patrick and he handed her a brown leather book that she raised in the air. "This is one of my first journals. In it, on about the tenth page, is a map for my life that I laid out eleven years ago. I was still wet behind the ears, thinking I could do anything. I was full of optimism and pride, with little reason to doubt myself. I titled this list, 'Ten Things to Do Before I Die.'

"The beautiful thing is, I accomplished every single wish on my list before this terminal diagnosis was confirmed in early June. Everything.

"I have traveled to Australia and Italy, been on an African safari, and swam with the dolphins. I've served in the Peace Corps, vacationed in Hawaii and Fiji, and married my soul mate. I was allowed to co-parent three godchildren who fortunately didn't have to live under my roof and endure my quirkiness full time."

Jillian laughed and blew a kiss to the three young girls, who were standing nearby with their parents. "I landed my dream job, shooting photos for *National Geographic*, and met Nelson Mandela and Oprah while on assignment," she said. "My favorite trip? To the Holy Land, where I bathed in God's presence.

"When I received the news that this cancer had gone undetected for so long that it was in the advanced stages, I pulled out this journal and re-read this list, which I drafted on my twenty-fifth birthday. I couldn't believe it when I checked off everything on it.

"Isn't that amazing, you guys? How many of us can say we've actually achieved some of our dreams, let alone all of them?"

Jillian paused to let the power of that reality sink in. She waved her finger. "I am human though," she said. "After I thanked God for granting me these blessings, I asked a huge favor. Couldn't I just change the title of the list from the 'Ten Things to Do Before I Die' to something else? Like, 'Ten Things to Do Before I Reach 40'? or 'Ten Things to Do Before My Hair Turns Gray'? I mean, come on, he didn't have to take it so literal!"

She chuckled, freeing everyone else to embrace the joke. The room erupted in laughter.

"I invited you here this evening to thank you for giving me the gift of you. Of your friendship. And your love."

Jillian searched the group and spoke to several people specifically. "Rachelle—we made mud pies and played jump rope and, before there was such a thing as AIDS, pricked our fingers and pressed them together so that we could be blood sisters. You kept my first secrets, helped me through my first broken heart, and even suffered punishment on my behalf rather than tell your mother that I was the one who ran through the living room and broke her favorite lamp."

Rachelle nodded and smiled, despite the tears spilling down her cheeks. How had she forgotten all of that? How had they let time, and other people, separate them?

"Amina, you guided me through college when I was this sheltered little girl who didn't realize there was a world outside of Philadelphia. Yolanda, just how did you snag our high school football star before I could?"

Another round of laughter filled the room, mingling with the flow of tears.

"Okay, okay, I guess I did pretty well myself. I'm keeping my man."

Jillian turned toward Patrick, who stood off to the side of the stage, watching her bask in the love radiating from the crowd. "Patrick, you have been the earth and wind to my fire; the ebony to my ivory; the true definition of a helpmate and soul mate. I love you."

She turned back to her friends. "I do have one request of each of you: Develop your own lists. Look at your lives and consider where you need to make adjustments. Life is way too short to take for granted or live halfheartedly. Do what you dream. God put the dream there. Promise me that as I move on to another phase, you'll give this part of your journey your best shot. That will be the best way to remember me, to honor our bond.

"To be honest with you, I am not ready to die. I'm just not ready. But I'm thankful that I am connected to God and I know where I'm going." Jillian paused and allowed a slow smile to spread across her face. "I'm thankful that I got to meet each of you and love you. I will leave here a happy woman, especially after the gift you have given me by showing up tonight.

"I am drinking in your presence," she said in a voice that had begun to tremble with emotion. "I'm going to tuck away this night in my memory and ask God to let me keep it, when I get to heaven."

Jillian's efforts to remain upbeat had been for naught. Rachelle took a tissue from a travel-size package that was circulating from hand to hand. Jillian's goddaughters ran to the stage and hugged her neck.

The youngest girl, who appeared to be five or six, flung her body across Jillian's lap and sobbed. Rachelle winced at the child's obvious fear and pain. Her mother came quickly and took the girl to a side room.

Jillian, who was visibly spent, raised the microphone to her lips a second time. She sighed. "This isn't easy—for the babies or any of us. But I really do want to celebrate the good and positive journey I've had. Will each of you come and give me a hug? Show me some love?"

Patrick rolled Jillian off the stage, over to a long table covered with a sea green tablecloth. She sat at the end of it, so that her friends could review the pictures of her life, from childhood in Philadelphia to her young adult years at Everson College in Jubilant, Texas, to the decade she traveled the world as a professional photographer.

Everyone except for Jillian's mother, brother, and sister, and several other relatives, formed a line so they could talk with her. As they waited their turn, they had time to peruse the informal photo gallery.

Rachelle, who grew up next door to Jillian and shared a dorm room with her when they went off to college, took in each of the images and felt the layers of time peeling away.

She remembered the backyard swing set captured in one of the photos and the teacup wallpaper that had graced the walls in Jillian's room until her sixteenth birthday.

She recalled their hangout spot on The Yard, the campus square at Everson College where freshmen and sophomores who didn't have transportation gathered most nights to socialize and flirt. There were graduation day photos and images of a party that followed later that evening, at the home of Rachelle's aunt and uncle, Charles and Irene, who lived near the campus.

Rachelle felt another wave of waterworks coming. What had happened to the youthful fervor her eyes possessed in those photos? It had never dimmed for Jillian, but somehow she had gotten off track.

Before she could formulate answers, it was her turn. Rachelle knelt before Jillian and hugged her gingerly.

Jillian grasped her tightly, cuing Rachelle that she wasn't fragile. She pulled back and stroked Rachelle's face. "Thanks for being here, Rae," she said softly, using the nickname she had given Rachelle when they were sixth graders and thought it was no longer cool to use their parent-given names. "It's so good to see you. The last time we talked we didn't agree on something really big. I don't know how that has worked out for you, but I heard through your mom that you were doing well and that your kids are beautiful. I hope you are happy."

Rachelle attempted a smile.

Jillian's eyes indicated that she understood. "Well, get happy, okay? For me and for you. You're living for both of us now. I've never stopped loving you like a sister, you know? Tell God your heart's desires. Trust him with all of them. That's the only reason all of this is okay—I learned how to do that when I was in Jerusalem."

Rachelle nodded. "I need to book a trip there; maybe it will clear out some of these emotional cobwebs."

Jillian shook her head. "That was my place of revelation, but it's different for everybody," she said. "You don't have to cross the world to find God. He's already with you. Just open up and let him in."

Rachelle hugged Jillian again.

"I love you, Jill, and I am so proud of you," Rachelle whispered in her ear. "I will tell my children about you and the beautiful person you've always been. I'll never forget you."

"I know you won't, Rachelle," Jillian said. "While I can, I will be praying for you."

When Rachelle walked away, the charge to "be happy" shook the chambers of her mind.

She thought about Gabe, who treated her like a piece in his art collection. She thought about her daily routine of playing the perfect wife, socializing with the proper friends and volunteering with the appropriate groups just often enough to make the city's socialite pages. In this moment, it struck her that her children were her only genuine source of joy.

Rachelle allowed herself to accept these realities tonight as she thought about Jillian's open charge to embrace truth and happiness. Was she up to this task?

On her way to the back of the dining room, she paused at a table where Amina, the college buddy she and Jillian had added to their crew freshman year, sat chatting with their high school friends, Yolanda and Marcus Drake.

The three of them stood and gave her a hug.

"Can you believe this?" Yolanda asked.

"Only because it's Jill," Rachelle said.

Amina nodded. "Only she could pull off something like this and leave her guests with a gift."

Rachelle decided to keep moving before she became a puddle of raw emotions again. "Stop by my table before you leave tonight so I can get your number and email address," she told Amina.

She turned toward the onetime teenage sweethearts, Yolanda and Marcus. "You two? I still keep track of you in Philly through my mother. Keep taking care of each other—you both look great."

Rachelle snaked through the rest of the tables until she reached her destination. Jillian's brother and sister sat with their petite, Vietnamese mother in the rear of the room at a table that gave them a clear view of Jillian but allowed other guests to be closer to her. Though each of them bore some resemblance to their now-deceased African American father, all of them, including Jillian, had their mother's eyes.

As Rachelle hugged Jillian's mother, she stroked the long ponytail that Mrs. Wright had worn for as long as Rachelle could remember. Mrs. Wright clung to her.

"Can you believe my baby?" She spoke quickly and softly, as if speed would diminish the thickness of her accent. "Who would throw a homegoing service before they leave earth, other than Jillian?"

Rachelle wiped a tear from her eye and laughed. She sat next to Mrs. Wright and draped her arm around the back of the woman's chair. "I've been thinking the same thing for the past few weeks—I believe everyone else here has too. But I'm glad she did this. I'm thankful that she gave me a chance to see her again."

Rachelle settled into her seat and feasted on dessert and conversation with Jillian's family for the rest of the evening. She felt heartsick about her friend's circumstances, but something else in her spirit was rumbling.

The simmering volcano shook her, because for the first time, she knew she couldn't ignore it. Not after what she had experienced tonight.

5

*R*achelle returned to her hotel room that evening determined to honor Jillian's request.

She slid out of her ankle-strap pewter pumps, pulled her cell phone from her evening bag, and perched on the end of the king-sized bed before flipping open the phone. She tapped the speed-dial code for her parents' number and closed her eyes.

She wanted to check on the kids and tell them goodnight, but she wasn't ready yet to inform them, or her mom and dad, that she was in San Diego with Jillian. Explaining everything that had occurred tonight would diminish some of its power.

Instead, she let Tate and Taryn do most of the talking.

"Did you feed Mel and Bob?" Tate wanted to make sure his fish weren't being neglected.

Rachelle sighed. "Yes, son. I sprinkled quite a bit of food in the tank yesterday, so they should be fine."

Gram had taken Taryn for her first manicure and the girl was beside herself. "We sat next to each other while we got our nails done. The lady who helped me said I could choose my polish color, and I wanted to put pink on one finger and purple on the next, but Gram wouldn't let me alternate. So I settled for the pink."

Rachelle inhaled to quash the resentment that threatened to

surface. She recalled her mother taking her for a manicure at about the same age and insisting that she get a "normal" pink polish, not the sparkly green she had wanted. Mom still had to control everything.

"When you come home, I'll do your nails in both colors," Rachelle told her daughter. "In the meantime, have fun and be good."

Rachelle ended the call with telephone kisses and took off the slate blue dress she had worn to Jillian's party. She carefully folded it and tucked it into her suitcase before pulling out her red silk pajamas and a gold silk scarf to wrap her hair in for the night. Her layered locks fell well below her shoulders, and it was a challenge to manage each night, but she found that when she wrapped her hair before lying on it, she had fewer split ends and tangles.

She stood in the bathroom under the bright lights and brushed her hair around and around her scalp, until finally it was all in place and she could secure it with the scarf. She brushed her teeth and hummed "Wind Beneath My Wings," the song that one of Jillian's friends from church had sung tonight, before the party ended.

Those tasks completed, she debated whether to take her shower first or get started on her list. The eagerness to look at her life won.

Rachelle turned off the light in the bathroom and settled in the hotel room's single sofa chair, next to a small round table positioned in front of windows that overlooked the city. From her twenty-first-floor position, the view was stunning. The pattern of night lights and intricate web of streets could have been a scene lifted from an artist's canvas.

San Diego was breathtaking. No wonder Jillian and Patrick had settled here. This seemed like a fitting place to find the inspiration to pursue one's dreams.

Rachelle stretched an arm to the middle of the table and grabbed the notepad and pen provided by the hotel. She wrote her title in big, loopy strokes: *Ten Things to Do Before I Turn 50.*

After witnessing Jillian's results, she wasn't going to play with death—she had children to raise. In a few months she would be thirty-six. That gave her fourteen years to accomplish whatever goals she outlined.

She sat there, however, and began to fidget. She was ready to brainstorm, but nothing surfaced. She numbered a sheet of paper from one to ten and waited.

Her thoughts turned to Tate and Taryn. In minutes, a dozen ideas of things she wanted to help her children accomplish flowed. Continuing their piano lessons and taking them to Florida to witness a space shuttle launch. Teaching them to appreciate all kinds of food and training them to do more chores.

Her thoughts even turned to Gabe, and what he would put on this list if he were here crafting it. He would be fifty in six years and by that time was hoping to spend at least one weekend a month on their boat. He wanted to be the head of the heart institute at St. Luke Episcopal Hospital and at a certain level with his private financial investments.

She had heard him share these plans with his golfing buddies and with his mother, before she died of a stroke. Rachelle had always been struck by the fact that while Gabe's father had been dead for ten years, Gabe still seemed to make choices based on what his dad expected of him. She often chided him for that habit, but tonight, she realized that whatever measure he was using to make decisions, he was a few steps ahead of her.

Rachelle returned her focus to the present, and checked the

numbers illuminated on the nearby digital clock. She had been sitting with her pen poised to write for nearly half an hour, but the page was still empty.

She knew what would be good for the kids. She could readily outline Gabe's goals, even though he hadn't articulated them to her directly. Yet, what did she want to achieve? What were her heart's burning desires?

She had to put something on paper. Anything. The white space beside the first number on the page mocked her.

"I want to . . ." Rachelle spoke the words aloud, certain that if she persisted, the answers would come. "I want to . . ."

She sighed. Everything she could dream up, she was already doing.

She didn't have to include travel on the list, because she vacationed often with Gabe and the kids or with her girlfriends. She didn't need to set financial goals, because the ones Gabe had were good enough for them both.

She was already at the perfect weight for her five-foot-six frame, and Pilates three times a week kept her toned. Her almond skin was healthy and blemish free, and she could shop at just about any store that caught her fancy.

Surely, though, she was missing something. How had Jillian managed to compile a list of things that mattered to her soul? Rachelle wished she were still tight enough with her friend to call her and ask.

Since that wasn't the case, she tried to imagine what Jillian would tell her, or would want to tell her, if they were having one of the candid girlfriend chats that used to be their norm. Jillian, she suspected, would suggest to her that when she had chosen to marry Gabe, she had chosen to put herself on the back burner, in favor of making sure his life reigned supreme.

Rachelle shook that thought from her mind and began writing.

1. Keep my optometry license current.

She sighed. This wasn't a first-time something to do before turning fifty, but at least it was a goal.

She had renewed the license every year since Tate's birth, thinking that someday she might decide to return to the profession she loved. Gabe had dismissed the idea as farfetched and unnecessary so many times that about five years ago, she began sending in her renewal fee to the state licensing board without telling him. She would not be able to officially practice again until she took a certain number of continuing education courses, but for now, just knowing her license was still in good standing helped her feel good about herself.

Rachelle stalled again. Only one thing on paper? This was ridiculous and frustrating.

She laid the pen and pad on the table and grabbed her pajamas on the way to the bathroom. She covered her head with a plastic cap, turned on the shower, and let the forceful stream of water warm up so she could step inside.

As she stood beneath its flow with her eyes closed and arms hugging her body, Rachelle's heart sank. How had her life come to this? If she couldn't set more than one personal goal for herself, she didn't really have a life. Now was the time to decide what, if anything, she was going to do about it.

6

The return flight home the next day was grueling.

A chain reaction of delays and overbooked airline seats kept Rachelle in the San Diego airport six hours past her scheduled arrival in Houston. Rachelle boarded her plane in the wee hours of the morning and slept for the most of the nonstop flight.

She had to get her bearings when she left the plane and entered the airport terminal just after seven a.m. Usually one of her friends, or Helen, her part-time housekeeper, swooped in to pick her up.

But Rachelle had given Helen the week off, since Gabe was away at his conference and the kids were in Philadelphia. After the series of unpredictable delays, she was glad she had decided to drive rather than bother Shelley, Trina, or Jade. One of them would have been happy to pick her up late last night, but those divas wouldn't be up this time of morning unless it was to go to and from one of their many exercise classes.

Rachelle retrieved her suitcase from baggage claim and rolled it out of the airport to the parking deck. The sun was positioning itself over the city, and she knew that soon, steamy heat would be rising from the pavement.

She slid her bag onto the backseat, settled behind the wheel, and fastened her seat belt. She turned the ignition and paused when Alicia Keys' voice permeated the Lexus with the lyrics to "Tell You Something."

Rachelle had been listening to the song frequently in the weeks leading up to her visit with Jillian and thinking about how accurate those words were—she did feel sorrow, and she wished she could better articulate to Jillian how much their friendship had meant. She didn't want it to end this soon, especially since they had just reconnected.

Rachelle tried to sing along, but her voice faded as the lump in her throat expanded. Why, of all the songs in her CD rotation, did she have to start the morning with this one? She rested her head on the steering wheel and sobbed. Jillian hadn't succumbed yet, but her frail appearance and the beautiful ceremony over the weekend left Rachelle with little doubt that it wouldn't be long.

They were the same age. Had similar hopes and dreams. They were good girls. So why was this happening? Jillian had even taken it a step further by deciding to live a life of full-fledged faith. Why was the God that she loved so much snatching her away so young?

Rachelle turned down the volume of the music and leaned back into the headrest. She wiped her eyes, reached for her cell phone, and called her mother. Mom wouldn't have answers to her questions, but because she knew Jillian, maybe she'd understand this distress. Plus, Rachelle couldn't think of anyone else who would be up this time of morning.

Rachelle wasn't surprised when her mother answered on the first ring.

"What's up, dear?"

Rachelle chuckled. "I should be asking you that," she said.

"What have you already accomplished this morning? It's just eight-something in Philly."

"Your dad and I are reading the paper and having breakfast," her mother responded. "The question is, what are *you* doing up this early?"

Rita Mitchell never ceased to amaze Rachelle. She was always quick on her feet, with astute questions or ready answers. Her calm demeanor and solid organizational skills seemed effortless. Rachelle routinely questioned why she struggled to accomplish that same level of competency, despite her role model.

"I just needed to hear your voice," Rachelle said.

"Is everything okay?" Rita asked.

Rachelle heard her children laughing in the background. She couldn't believe they were up so early. Mom must have enforced an early bedtime.

"Jillian's dying, Mom."

Her mother gasped.

"I just returned from a farewell gathering she hosted in San Diego, and I . . . I don't know. It's hitting me harder than I expected."

Rachelle waited for the comforting words she needed to hear right now. She crossed her fingers that Mom would come through and offer a dose of reassurance that despite Jillian's circumstances, everything would turn out okay.

"I haven't seen Jillian's mother in a while. I didn't know," Rita said. "The family must be devastated. What's wrong? What's the diagnosis?"

Rachelle explained that Jillian had breast cancer and described the life celebration she had hosted.

"Why didn't you tell me about this? I would have gone with you, Rachelle. At least to pay my respects."

Rachelle stiffened. "Mom, this wasn't a funeral. There aren't 'respects' to pay—not yet. This was a chance to say goodbye but also to tell her how much we love her. It was just hard. Besides, you have Tate and Taryn. You couldn't have accompanied me."

Rachelle sighed. Why had she thought her mother would understand?

"Well, it is indeed sad," Rita said. "But get yourself together, Rachelle. Sounds like Jillian has accepted this. It's good that you had a chance to say goodbye. You'll be fine.

"What are you doing now, with all of this free time on your hands? Have you heard from Gabe since he left?"

Rachelle closed her eyes. That was just like her mother, to say her two cents' worth about an uncomfortable subject, then turn the discussion elsewhere. Rachelle inhaled and exhaled slowly a few times to ease her tense muscles. She had seen Gabe advise many a stressed-out friend or acquaintance to use this technique to lower their blood pressure or reduce the anxiety that contributed to heart problems. Not that she had either of those health issues—she had long ago adopted the strategy to keep her cool in trying situations, and now it was almost a reflex.

"Mom, let me call you and the kids back later, okay? Tell Dad I said hello."

Rachelle tucked the cell phone into her purse and put the car in reverse. Before she backed out of the parking space, she pressed the FM radio control on her steering column.

She didn't listen to the radio often, but today, she felt restless. She wanted something other than the dozens of songs on her CDs and iPod that she played so often she could sing them in her sleep. She surfed stations until the strains of a melody caught her ear:

"Grateful, grateful, grateful; Gratefulness . . . is flowing from my heart . . ."

When the song wound to a close, the DJ piped up. "Good Sunday morning, Houstonians! That was Hezekiah Walker and the Love Fellowship Choir with the beautiful song, 'Grateful.' What are you grateful for this morning?"

Rachelle focused on the digital radio panel as if the DJ were speaking specifically to her.

"Let me ask you another question based on a Hezekiah-inspired song," he said. "Who do you need to survive? Yes family, yes friends, but have you tried God?"

Normally, this would be the point at which she tuned out or turned the dial. This morning, however, her heart was tender.

Rachelle pulled out of the parking deck and sat at a traffic light a block away from the Sam Houston Tollway. She could take the freeway to her cushy suburb, but why go home? No one was there.

Her friends would be spending time with their husbands and kids today. Since she had neither of those to make it a family affair, she'd be a tagalong.

Rachelle glanced at the dashboard clock and noted that it was just eight a.m. The red-eye flight and multiple cups of coffee over the last hour had left her wired. Why not hit the road?

She could be at Alanna's place in Dallas before her sister climbed out of bed, around noon . . . or maybe she should drive just over two hours to Jubilant and spend a few days with Aunt Irene and Uncle Charles. The surprise would make their day, and she realized in answer to the radio announcer's question, they were among the people she needed and cherished most, even though she hadn't regularly expressed her affection over the last dozen years.

Gabe felt threatened by her visits to her college town and to Aunt Irene and Uncle Charles's home for reasons he had never fully articulated. The few times he had accompanied her before and after they wed, he hadn't relaxed enough to enjoy himself. Rachelle soon realized that unless they were unwinding or having fun in a formal or structured activity that in the long run furthered Gabe's career goals, her husband didn't care to participate.

This morning she thought about her anorexic list of things she wanted to accomplish in the coming years. She had dated the paper, folded it up, and tucked it in her wallet, so that when ideas came to her, she could readily fill the nine blank slots.

Visiting her extended family didn't necessarily belong on the list of long-term goals, but it was something she wanted to do, and for the first time in a long time, she didn't feel the need to justify her desire. Gabe wasn't here to shift the excitement she was feeling about her Sunday morning excursion into doubt about whether her relatives cared to be bothered with her. She knew differently.

Fresh from her visit with Jillian, now was the perfect time to immerse herself in Aunt Irene and Uncle Charles's world. They would accept her as is, even if, in her quest to create a list of tangible goals, she stopped being the Rachelle who lived to please everybody but herself.

7

The redbrick church looked smaller each time Rachelle returned.

Maybe it was because of the volume of megachurches sprouting up around Houston. Everything looked miniature in comparison to some of those structures.

The rich harmonies that floated across the summer wind from the choir loft more than compensated for the building's modest appearance. Music filled Rachelle's ears as soon as she stepped out of her sedan. These folks weren't having church, they were having *chuch*.

She locked the car door with her key chain control and crossed the gravel parking lot. The enthusiastic welcome from the salt-and-pepper afroed usher who greeted her made the steep climb up the steps to the St. Peter's Baptist Church sanctuary worthwhile.

Aunt Irene and Uncle Charles must be inside somewhere. She had stopped by their house when she arrived in Jubilant, but realized when no one answered the door that they were already at church.

Rachelle glanced at a clock in the foyer while she waited to be admitted into the worship service. 11:05 a.m. She hadn't missed much.

She gave herself a once-over. Changing clothes in the bathroom at the local McDonald's hadn't been ideal, but the lightly wrinkled black slacks and silver satin top would have to do. In Houston, dressy casual had become the norm for churchgoers. Smaller cities didn't always catch on as fast, but she hoped she wouldn't embarrass her aunt and uncle.

Rachelle peered through the small, rectangular windowpanes of the doors that led into the sanctuary. An usher stood on each side, preventing anyone from entering until instructed to do so. The youth choir sang and swayed to an upbeat version of the hymn, "Down at the Cross." Most of the congregation was on its feet, accompanying them.

Rachelle scanned each row, trying to determine where Aunt Irene might be sitting. It was hard to pinpoint her in the sea of bobbing heads and waving hands.

The scene brought back memories from Rachelle's days as a student at Everson College. Though she had sporadically attended church growing up, her participation in the Baptist Student Union Choir at Everson came with mandatory weekly Bible studies and with numerous engagements in churches throughout Jubilant and surrounding cities. Soon, she and some of her friends from the choir had begun attending a small church close to campus, whose members' expressions of faith mirrored these parishioners, from the closed eyes and movement to the music, to the arms reaching toward heaven and outbursts of gratitude.

When Pastor Taylor motioned for the congregation to be seated, an usher allowed her to enter and another beckoned her forward.

"I'm looking for Irene and Charles Burns," Rachelle whispered.

The older woman searched faces in each aisle and led Rachelle to a seat in the third row. Everyone in the pew turned toward her, including Aunt Irene and her youngest daughter, Yasmin. Aunt Irene's eyes widened.

She almost looks startled, Rachelle thought.

Aunt Irene and Yasmin moved closer together to make room for Rachelle on the cushioned pew. When she took her seat, she noticed that Irene's older daughter, Indigo, wasn't with them, and she didn't see the girl in the choir loft filled with teenagers.

Yasmin hugged Rachelle's waist when Rachelle settled next to her.

"Where are Taryn and Tate?" the girl whispered.

"In Philadelphia, with their Gram and Poppa," Rachelle said.

She patted Yasmin's hand when the girl's face fell. At seven she was a year younger than Taryn, but the girls loved each other dearly. Though they were cousins, the resemblance between them was striking. Both had flowing hair like their mothers, brown sugar complexions, and prominent jaw lines. People who saw the girls together often mistook them for sisters, an error that delighted them.

They saw little of each other because of Rachelle's infrequent visits to Jubilant, but the few times the girls had been together, they spent every waking moment bonding.

Can we call Taryn later so I can say hi? Yasmin scribbled the message on the back of her church bulletin in pink gel ink.

Rachelle smiled and nodded. She looked past Yasmin at Aunt Irene, whose lips were pursed.

Aunt Irene's eyes darted to and fro as she scanned the pulpit. She made eye contact with Uncle Charles, who sat near the front on a pew reserved for church trustees that offered a full view of the congregation. She motioned in Rachelle's direction with a jerk of her head.

Rachelle took it all in and frowned. Aunt Irene noticed her attentiveness and turned on a smile.

"Good to see you," she mouthed silently to Rachelle.

The choir finished the hymn with a flourish and Rev. Taylor approached the podium. "Please bow your heads and join me in prayer," he said.

When Rachelle opened her eyes after the "Amen," she caught Aunt Irene peering at her again. Rachelle leaned past Yasmin so she could whisper in her aunt's ear. "Is everything okay?"

Before Aunt Irene could respond, Pastor Taylor cleared his throat and asked for everyone's attention.

"As St. Peter's members know, we've been without a music director for some time, since Sister Hightower and her family moved to Delaware. God has blessed us with some stellar candidates for the position, and during last month's church meeting, we voted to hire the young man who joins us today. This gentleman not only knows music inside and out and plays piano and drums, the brother can also sing, y'all!"

Rachelle chuckled along with the rest of the congregation. There was nothing like a man who could hold a tune. During her years with the Baptist Student Union Choir, she had seen many a church sister swoon over the brothers who sang solos with passion and fervor. From Pastor Taylor's description, it appeared that might happen today.

"What makes this young man even more special is that he and I have a special bond," Pastor Taylor said. "As I've previously mentioned, I met him about ten years ago, when I was pastor of a church in Milwaukee. He and his family became members, and he soon was blessing us with his gifted voice.

"The fact that he and I have reconnected, in the city where he attended college, shows you how incredible God is at bringing people together in his own timing," Pastor Taylor said. "We'll have him here part time to help our music department flourish, but the real reason he has come back to Jubilant is to work at his alma mater. Everson College recruited him as a fellow for the engineering department, where he'll serve on the faculty.

"This young man is smart, he has integrity, and he loves the Lord. Everybody stand to your feet and welcome St. Peter's new director of music, Troy Hardy!"

Rachelle's hands froze in mid-clap. Breath flew from her body. Troy Hardy. *Her* Troy Hardy?

She plopped down, onto the cushioned pew, while the new church staff member received an enthusiastic welcome. Aunt Irene sat down too and leaned over to her.

"I'm sorry," she said into Rachelle's ear as the thunderous applause and cheers surrounded them. "I didn't know you were coming. I was planning to tell you. You okay?"

Rachelle's eyes were fixed on Aunt Irene, but her mind was replaying images of fourteen years earlier: that wilting bouquet of yellow roses. The thin gold band she had used her meager savings to buy. The love that overflowed from her heart to her handsome young husband—Troy Antonio Hardy.

All these years later, her long-ago choices still had the power to sting. As the men and women around her settled down, she had a clear view of him.

He was still movie-star gorgeous. Same broad smile and quiet strength. Lifting weights was clearly still a hobby, because his muscles strained to fit comfortably inside the arms of his collared shirt and blue suit jacket. His golden complexion seemed unmarred by time or life's woes. The shaved head suited him.

Rachelle's heart double dutched. She inhaled deeply to stifle the tears that threatened to surface. The emotion surprised her, given that she had been married to someone else for more than a decade.

But Troy would always be the first man she loved, no matter how badly Gabe, or her parents, wanted to erase him from her past. She would always be linked to him because of a series of first experiences that only he had shared with her.

Rachelle shook her head to clear her thoughts. Here she was in Jubilant, trying to get away from all that had been troubling her recently, trying to figure out what kind of life she wanted in the years to come, and she had run smack-dab into one of her lifetime regrets.

She sat facing the man who might hold the key to her happiness. He was the one person with whom she had experienced an inexplicable joy and sense of purpose. Why had she let him go?

Rachelle lowered her eyes and gazed at her left hand, at her ring finger. The four-carat diamond Gabe had given her last year for their tenth wedding anniversary sparkled. It left no room for misunderstandings. She was very married.

She looked up at Troy and sighed. People took God too seriously sometimes. The Man upstairs obviously had a sense of humor. Right now, though, laughter didn't seem fitting.

Since traveling back in time wasn't an option, Rachelle needed an escape plan. She had left Troy once before, against her wishes. Today, she pondered how quickly she could manage if it were her mission.

8

*R*egardless of the history between them, Rachelle had to give Troy his propers. The boy was on fire.

He thanked the congregation for the warm welcome and assured them he was not only joining the staff but would soon become a member of the church.

"I'm looking forward to being a part of St. Peter's ministry and mission," Troy said, to a swell of applause from members. "The Bible contains numerous references to music and its significance in ministering to God's leaders and his people. We can't underestimate the power of a God-inspired hymn or gospel song to lift someone's spirit, help him or her connect with the heavenly Father, or give him or her answers to questions they've been wrestling with.

"I'm praying that we can take St. Peter's awesome choirs to a new level of excellence, to the glory of God," Troy said. "Let's work together to make it happen."

Troy turned toward the church's pianist, drummer, and saxophonist, and they began playing the opening strains of an upbeat song. He raised the microphone to his lips, reared back his head, and uttered, "The presence of the Lord is here . . ."

By the time the song wound to an end, after several encores, there wasn't a dry eye in the church. Troy gave the microphone back to Pastor Taylor and left the pulpit to sit on one of the front pews. He bowed his head, as if in prayer, while the men and women who sat nearby reached over to pat his shoulder.

The song touched Rachelle, not only because she was hearing Troy's moving tenor again, but also because she still had Jillian's counsel on her mind. Be happy. Live fully. Love God. The lyrics expressed joy over God's willingness to dwell among and bless people who love him. This song was the musical equivalent of Jillian's message.

With the way she had been feeling—and behaving—over the past month, the song left her out of sorts. Going through the motions at home had been frustrating. Searching for answers this past weekend had been unsettling. And now, sitting here in church, she felt hollow.

The blank Ten Things to Do list in her purse served as a searing reminder of how little she knew about herself when, by all appearances, she led a picture-perfect life.

As Pastor Taylor encouraged adults and children in the congregation to give God a try, Rachelle contemplated how to ease out of the sanctuary without Troy seeing her.

"It's not about coming here and sitting in the pews on Sunday, really it's not," Pastor Taylor said. "It's about using this place as a vehicle to form a relationship with the one who gives you life and breath, the one who gives you new chances every day."

After his plea, ushers approached each pew with offering plates and Rachelle gave up on slipping out of the service. She didn't want to embarrass her aunt and uncle by leaving at an inappropriate juncture or by appearing stingy.

Pastor Taylor prayed over the offering, then invited Troy to share a few more words before the service ended.

Rachelle hadn't noticed a young girl sitting next to him until she stood and went forward with him. He clutched her hand and the two of them faced the congregation.

"Everyone, this is Chaundra," he said.

"Hi, Chaundra!" the congregation bellowed.

The girl, who appeared to be about thirteen, looked at Troy and smiled before waving and tucking her head down. With a short bob, wire-rimmed glasses, thin legs, and a dusting of freckles across her fair skin, she didn't resemble him, but she was cute.

Rachelle held her breath, waiting for him to introduce a wife. *I can handle it, I can handle it.*

Instead, he hugged the girl and blessed everyone with a megawatt smile. "The two of us are thankful to be embraced by this church family. We don't take your cheers of support or the graciousness you've shown since we arrived here last week from Milwaukee for granted. As we settle in, please keep us in your prayers. And for you other little ladies out there, feel free to help Chaundra out. She'll have a better time learning about her new city and new school if you girls teach her, instead of her having to rely on me."

Pastor Taylor walked to the lectern and motioned for the congregation to rise for the benediction. Before he could speak, his wife waved at him and mouthed instructions. Rachelle's heart sank. She knew what was coming.

"Oh, yes," Pastor Taylor said, acknowledging his forgetfulness. "In all of our excitement over Troy, we didn't welcome our visitors! Does anyone have a special guest today?"

Aunt Irene looked at Rachelle. When Rachelle shook her head, Aunt Irene sat back in the pew. But Yasmin tugged at her arm.

"You haven't visited in a long time, Cousin Rachelle," Yasmin said. "You're a friend. Stand up. Say something."

"Not today." Rachelle spoke softly because a couple behind her were introducing themselves.

She thought she was safe when several other churchgoers made comments and took their seats, but Pastor Taylor clearly didn't miss a thing.

"Sister Irene, I see you've got someone with you. Care to introduce her?"

Aunt Irene coughed and stood. "Well, Pastor, just a relative visiting from Houston. She went to college here in Everson and has come to service before with our family, so she's more of a friend than a visitor . . . and she's shy."

I love you, Aunt Irene.

Rachelle hoped the message reached her aunt telepathically and that Pastor Taylor could read through the lines—she didn't want to get up and speak.

It didn't work.

"We won't bite," he said to Rachelle. "Stand up, ma'am!"

All eyes were on Rachelle as she peeled herself from the pew and smoothed her slacks. She took a deep breath and focused on Pastor Taylor, since he was the one intent on unwittingly humiliating her.

"Good afternoon, church. My name is Rachelle Covington. I bring you greetings from Houston, Texas . . ." Her voice trailed off. One usually inserted the name of his or her church and pastor at this point. Since she had an affiliation with neither, she was at a loss. "Ah . . . it's always a pleasure to worship here with my Aunt Irene and Uncle Charles, and I pray that the rest of this week will be blessed for each of you."

Rachelle sat down quickly, but couldn't help glancing at Troy. He had turned around in his seat, and his mouth was hanging open.

While Pastor Taylor closed the service, Troy's eyes remained fixed on Rachelle. Rather than animosity or longing, she detected an emotion she couldn't decipher.

Years ago, she knew what his every twitch or facial tic meant. Now, although the face and voice hadn't changed much, she didn't know him at all.

She wondered why his wife wasn't with him today. He hadn't even mentioned her, and there wasn't a band on his ring finger. Maybe he was a single father. The more she mused, the more her curiosity mushroomed.

Before he decided to move in her direction and ask her similar questions about her personal life, Rachelle grabbed her purse. She turned to Aunt Irene and hugged her.

"Mind if I leave now and head over to your place?"

Aunt Irene pulled her key ring from her purse, twisted off a key, and handed it over. "I understand," she said and looked toward Troy, who had been swamped by well-wishers. "You're staying over, aren't you? Take Reuben's bedroom. He was supposed to come home this weekend, but with him, there's no telling. College has driven him temporarily insane. He calls when he needs money and comes home when every stitch of clothing needs to be washed."

Aunt Irene and Rachelle laughed.

Rachelle didn't think her cousin Reuben had the same issues, but when she had left Philadelphia for Jubilant, she remembered being grateful to have some freedom for the first time. Mom had still called several times a week to make sure she was studying and staying out of trouble at Everson, but at least she hadn't been able to hover and tell her what to wear or whom to hang out with.

"Yasmin, coming with me?"

59

The girl looked at Rachelle, and then over her shoulder, toward a group of girls her age. They waved her over.

Rachelle laughed. "I see—I'm not going to win the popularity contest today," she told Yasmin. "Go on—be with your friends. I'll see you at the house."

Yasmin dashed off and Aunt Irene shook her head.

"That girl is something else," she said. "Busy as a bee, but a sweetheart. You can tell me later how your babies are doing."

Rachelle promised to give her an update on Tate and Taryn just as one of Aunt Irene's friends approached and hugged her from behind.

"We missed you the other night at the women's tea! Where were you, Irene?"

Rachelle seized the opportunity to escape and waved goodbye to Aunt Irene. She scanned the crowd on her way out of the sanctuary. Uncle Charles had disappeared. He must be in the church office with the other deacons, counting the offering. She snaked her way through the socializing parishioners and paused once she reached the foyer. Before she stepped outside the church, she looked back and caught a glimpse of Troy approaching Aunt Irene with open arms so he could envelop her in a hug.

Rachelle rummaged through her purse for her car keys and fought the surging anger. Aunt Irene and Uncle Charles were church leaders; they had to have known for a while that Troy was under consideration for the position at St. Peter's. Why hadn't one of them said something?

She felt like she was in college again, when everyone was deciding what was best for her, without including her in the process. This time around, she wasn't going to be so easy to manipulate. She had an agenda of her own.

9

*R*achelle had driven full speed into a personal storm with no warning.

"Maybe I should leave," she said to Alanna. She sat on Reuben's bed, talking softly into her cell phone in case Aunt Irene or Uncle Charles ventured past the closed door.

"You gonna let a man run you out of town? You're better than that, Chelle," Alanna said. "Just calm down. I know it's unsettling for Troy to be there, but it's been fifteen years. You can't still have feelings for him, can you?"

Rachelle didn't respond. Alanna knew better.

"Well, you haven't talked about him in a long, long time, so I thought you had moved on. I thought you were happy with Gabe—until the stunt you pulled last week before he left town," Alanna said. "You can't leave Jubilant, though. You know how much Aunt Irene and Uncle Charles love you. They would be hurt."

Maybe they would understand, since they were concerned enough to keep the news of Troy's arrival from me, Rachelle thought. "If this were you, what would you do?"

Alanna sighed. "Why are you always asking me how I would handle something? I'm supposed to look to you for advice. You know me—I would have split the second church was over, girl."

The sisters laughed, but Rachelle's spirits sagged. Why had she never had that kind of courage?

"You could do it and get away with it too," Rachelle said. "Me? I'd be accused of causing family trauma, drama, and a whole range of other issues if I had done that today."

"If you need to leave to be okay, Rachelle, I say do it," Alanna said. "You gotta take care of you, whether others understand or not."

Rachelle bit her tongue. *The rules aren't the same.*

Alanna had always made her needs a priority and had spoken her mind without hesitation, and no one batted an eye. Her breathtaking beauty and engaging personality bought her breaks others couldn't pay cash for.

"Let me get off this phone and go outside," Rachelle said. "Guests are arriving for the barbecue, and I better help."

"See, there you go," Alanna said.

"What do you mean?"

"Did anybody ask you to help? If not, why are you feeling obligated? You're a guest too. Go on out there and chill! I'll call you back in a couple of hours to see if you're feeling better."

Rachelle smiled. Alanna kept her in line.

Her baby sister couldn't get her love life straight or figure out what career she wanted to pursue long term, but the bachelor's degree in French and master's in marketing allowed her to keep landing great jobs throughout metro Dallas. If she'd only stay somewhere longer than a year and a half and stop searching for Mr. Right in all the wrong places, she just might be all right.

"Thanks, sis," Rachelle said. She still hadn't told Alanna about Jillian. This Troy thing had thrown her for a loop. "I'll catch you up on some other things soon. Love ya."

Rachelle placed the cell phone on the maple dresser and left the bedroom. She sauntered down the hallway leading from the bedroom to the kitchen, taking in the numerous framed photos that lined the wall. There were images of her and Alanna when they were young girls, visiting Aunt Irene and Uncle Charles one summer.

Pictures of Aunt Irene and Uncle Charles that had been taken before they became parents were interspersed with images of extended family members and close friends. Rachelle giggled at some of the photos, especially the ones of Uncle Charles leaning against a teal car that Rachelle thought resembled an iron submarine.

He really thought he was fine.

She strolled into the kitchen, where Aunt Irene was making potato salad. Aunt Irene had come home from church and launched right into preparing food for the cookout. She paused and smiled at Rachelle.

"I'm so glad you surprised us today. It does my heart good to see you. You look as pretty as always. Are you eating anything?"

Rachelle laughed. "Yes, Auntie, I'm eating. I also exercise just about every day—jogging and Pilates. Keeps me looking my best."

Aunt Irene shook her head. "I tell you, you young women come up with some stuff. I never pretended that I was going to be a cover girl when I was your age, so I ate what I wanted." She patted her hips. "Now I've got some regrets, but hey, I wasn't denying myself something I wanted to enjoy. I'll be sixty this year, and you can bet that I'm not worried about my figure."

Rachelle smiled. Aunt Irene had full cheeks and wide hips, but Uncle Charles didn't seem to be complaining. She was still a pretty woman, and Rachelle was sure that men her age still considered her someone to talk about.

"Fried food is my big no-no," Rachelle said. "I'm married to a cardiothoracic surgeon, after all. Other than that, I just try to eat in moderation. The exercise gives me energy and just helps me feel better."

Aunt Irene stuck a tablespoon in the potato salad and took a bite. "Hmm, this is so good," she said. "I'm glad you've got a system for staying healthy, baby. Want some potato salad?"

Rachelle shook her head. "Not right now, but I'll take it out and put it on the table if you want me to."

"It's too hot out there for it right now. I'll refrigerate it and bring it out when it's time to bless all of the food," Aunt Irene said. "Go on out and get a cool drink. Say hi to your uncle."

Rachelle stepped outside, into the backyard, and remembered why she spent most of her summer days at a spa or indoor pool. Sweat trickled down her back before she had taken a good three steps toward Uncle Charles.

It was about three p.m. and the day couldn't have been hotter. Here she was at a Sunday afternoon barbecue in July. In southern Texas. The humidity left her longing for a bath filled with ice cubes.

"Stop complaining," Uncle Charles said and motioned for her to sit in the lawn chair next to him. "Don't you rich folk cook out in your hoity-toity section of Houston?"

Rachelle laughed and swatted him with the newspaper he had placed in her lap, along with a few ears of corn to shuck.

"Yeah," she teased back, "on our air-conditioned patios."

She grabbed her thick mane and pulled a hair claw from the pocket of the khaki shorts she had found in her suitcase. Today was a testament to why packing more than she thought she needed could be beneficial. And thank goodness she kept a few extra supplies in the glove compartment of her car for Taryn's hair emergencies. If she didn't get this stuff off her neck, she might be tempted to cut it.

After shucking the corn, Rachelle and Uncle Charles moved their chairs under one of several white tents where they could relax. He sipped a soda while she chug-a-lugged a bottle of water.

A heavy silence settled between them, until finally, he spoke.

"We shoulda told you about Troy, but we just didn't know how," Uncle Charles said. "Knowing how much went on between you two, it was hard when we learned he was moving back to Jubilant and wanted the director of music position. But he was the best candidate of the bunch, and we believe God sent him to us."

Rachelle peered through the haze of heat at the neighborhood kids playing in the shallow pool Uncle Charles had inflated for them. Yasmin was frolicking with them and orchestrating teams for a water game.

"I'm not questioning your commitment to follow God, Uncle Charles," she said. "I just want to know why, once it was clear that Troy was a contender for the job, you or Aunt Irene didn't pick up the phone and call me. I had a right to know. I make sporadic visits to Jubilant; and I occasionally go to your church. Just the fact that he moved back to Texas meant there was a chance of me running into him. You should have prepared me for that."

Uncle Charles sipped his soda and shrugged. He looked away before he spoke. "I don't know, Rachelle. We knew how hard you took it when you two broke up. We just weren't sure what to do."

"No," Rachelle said in as even a tone as she could muster. "We didn't 'break up.' My parents gave me an ultimatum—get a divorce or find a way to pay for optometry school on my own. I think that could be considered blackmail instead of a 'breakup.'"

Uncle Charles cleared his throat and rose from the seat. He

patted her shoulder, and wandered away, toward Yasmin and her friends.

Rachelle could tell she had crossed his line of tolerance. Aunt Irene often accused him of fleeing from uncomfortable situations.

Rachelle sat there awhile longer, stewing over the circumstances. More guests began to arrive, and she realized she needed to give the subject a rest. *But I always do that—give it a rest; keep the peace; make sure no feathers are ruffled. What if I don't feel like it?*

Before she could mull over answers, a startling thought crossed her mind: Troy might have been invited to this barbecue before her family knew she'd be there. If he showed up, she was pulling an "Alanna"—she would pack up and be home by nightfall.

10

*S*ince Uncle Charles went in one direction, Rachelle chose to go in the other.

She gathered the ears of corn she had shucked and cradled them in her arms. Before Uncle Charles could grill them, they needed to be washed, and she might as well do the honors.

When she reached the patio that led to the kitchen, Rachelle noticed Aunt Irene standing under a nearby tree, gulping from a red plastic cup. Aunt Irene smiled when Rachelle approached her and tucked her hand with the cup behind her back.

"What's up?" she asked. She squirmed under Rachelle's curious gaze. "This heat makes you thirsty, doesn't it?"

Rachelle nodded and peered over her aunt's shoulder. The cup held a clear liquid and was half full, but why would Aunt Irene try to hide it?

"Is that 'happy juice' or something?"

Rachelle laughed, but Aunt Irene winked at her.

"I need a little help to unwind sometimes," she said. "Between getting ready for this barbecue/birthday party for Indigo and dealing with your stubborn uncle and my creaky hip, Lord knows I need something!"

She leaned closer. "But don't tell anybody, okay? Let's keep this between us. Come on, help me set the rest of the food out and bring out Indigo's cake."

Rachelle wanted to pinch herself. She had to be dreaming. All of her aunts and uncles were social drinkers except Aunt Irene, who had always said she didn't partake so she could remain clearheaded enough to hear from God. When had that changed, and why? Rachelle followed Aunt Irene into the kitchen, but decided not to question her until later, when they had some time alone.

Before she could fret further, Aunt Melba barreled in with a friend trailing her. Bags that overflowed with chips, two-liter sodas, and ice filled their arms. Aunt Melba's face was nearly hidden by her packages, but her hearty laugh was unmistakable.

"I'm here now! Let's get this party started!"

Melba had never been one to use an "inside voice." Family gatherings weren't half as lively when she wasn't around, and everyone teased her about it.

"Shoot, I was the middle child—I had to fight to get some attention," she'd always respond. "That saying is the truth—the squeaky wheel gets the oil, and I don't like being rusty or ashy!"

"A little coarse sometimes, yes; but never 'rusty or ashy,'" Rachelle's mother had commented years ago, after one of Melba's weekend visits to Philadelphia.

Other than Rita Mitchell, no one seemed to mind Melba's volume or straightforwardness. She was colorful and flamboyant and lovable. She was also gorgeous. At five foot ten, she was slender, but thick in all the right places. She wore a short-layered haircut that accentuated her bronze complexion and high cheekbones.

Aunt Irene was the baby sister and Rachelle's dad was the oldest of the three children, but Aunt Melba looked nowhere near the sixty-two years she insisted her birth certificate documented.

When she visited Houston for shopping trips to the Galleria and other exclusive stores, strangers often mistook her for Rachelle's older sister.

Rachelle still couldn't fathom why Aunt Melba hadn't fled Jubilant as a teenager for the runways of New York or Paris.

Melba, Irene, and Rachelle's dad, Herbert, loved each other deeply, which meant that loving each other's children was second nature. Since Melba had never had any of her own, she claimed Rachelle, Alanna, and Irene's crew by default.

Aunt Melba set her grocery bags on the granite countertop, next to Irene, who was arranging deviled eggs on a serving tray. She kissed her sister's cheek, then turned toward Rachelle.

"Well, look what the cat drug in. When did you get here, Rachelle?"

Rachelle grinned and trotted over for a hug. "It's great to see you, Aunt Melba. I made a surprise visit this morning. Gabe is away on business and the kids are with Mom and Dad for the month, so I thought I'd drive down."

Melba raised an eyebrow and grabbed a deviled egg. "Gabe's away, so you can play?" She popped the appetizer into her mouth and waited.

Rachelle smiled but didn't respond. Aunt Melba had always been able to illuminate the heart of matters. Maybe that's why her hair salon remained the busiest in town. It wasn't unusual for clients who had moved away to drive several hours to Jubilant for a special occasion appointment with Melba.

Rachelle couldn't blame them. Melba was indeed a fabulous hairstylist, but her unparalleled energy, doses of encouragement, and the tell-it-like-it-is advice she doled out were the true magnets. Melba didn't play favorites—whoever sat in her chair had her full attention.

Rachelle turned to the woman who had accompanied her aunt. "Hi, I'm Rachelle."

"Hello, Rachelle." The woman smiled and extended her hand. "I'm Cynthia, one of Melba's clients and also a friend. Nice to meet you."

Rachelle wondered how Cynthia had been roped into attending the barbecue. Either she was new to town, in a crisis, or had struck Melba's fancy as someone the family would appreciate knowing.

"Good people need to know other good people" was a Melba catchphrase.

"This is Doctor Cynthia Bridgeforth, pediatrician extraordinaire," Melba said, satisfying Rachelle's curiosity. "Could be living the cushy life of a private practice doctor caring for Jubilant's well-to-do kids and instead spends her days in the toughest part of town, helping the children most folks gave up on before they even got here. This Cynthia, she's something else."

Rachelle was intrigued. Before she could ask questions, though, the birthday girl made her entrance with an entourage of lip-gloss–smothered, giggling friends. The various perfumes and scented lotions they wore overshadowed the baked beans Aunt Irene had retrieved from the oven.

While today's gathering was a celebration of Indigo's fifteenth birthday, it also was enough reason for the family and their extensive circle of friends to fellowship. Most teenagers shied away from social functions that included embarrassing adults, but Indigo seemed to be dodging that pattern. Aunt Irene and Uncle Charles had made it a practice to surround all three children with loved ones at every turn. They might never know the meaning of the term *nuclear family*.

Indigo parted the crowd and ran to embrace Rachelle. "You came to my party but you didn't bring my little cousins?"

She rested her skinny arms on Rachelle's shoulders and locked eyes with her. Rachelle laughed.

"When did you get so tall? And why weren't you at church today?"

"I slept over at my friend Sabrina's house last night." Indigo pointed to the girl. "But if I had known the new director of music was going to show up today and sing, I might have popped in. 'Shawty' is fine!"

Indigo and her giggling girlfriends moved as one force toward the back door and tumbled outside. Rachelle couldn't help but smile, despite hearing Indigo refer to Troy in that fashion. She was just an infant when everything transpired between Rachelle and Troy during their college days and didn't know that this "Shawty" was her former cousin by marriage.

Aunt Melba winked at Rachelle and grabbed the baked beans. Cynthia picked up the tray of deviled eggs and the two women followed the girls outside.

The mention of her ex-husband reminded Rachelle of a pertinent concern. "Is . . . Troy . . . coming to the barbecue, Aunt Irene? Did you invite him?"

Aunt Irene averted her eyes. She wet a dishtowel and concentrated on wiping the island countertop. "He was invited, along with a few other folks from church. But he came up to me after service this afternoon and told me that he and Chaundra were having dinner with Pastor and First Lady Taylor and might not have time to stop by."

Rachelle fiddled with the paper napkins she had folded into triangles. "Did he . . . ask about me?"

"He saw you, Rachelle," Aunt Irene said. "I saw him looking at you. But he didn't say a word to me about you."

Ouch. Why did that sting? Hadn't they both moved on? She had fled church to avoid him, so her disappointment surprised her.

She was curious about what he'd been doing all these years since they split and how he had wound up back in Jubilant. Aunt Irene probably knew everything, but Rachelle decided not to ask.

An awkward silence filled the kitchen and Rachelle took that as her cue. She grabbed a serving spoon and an aluminum pan filled with potato salad and headed for the door.

She crossed the expansive lawn and placed the food on a cloth-covered table under one of the tents. A couple Rachelle didn't know sat nearby under a tree, chatting. The woman leaned into the man and he bent down to kiss her nose.

"No newlywed hanky panky. Y'all got little eyes watching ya!" Uncle Charles yelled from across the patio, where he was basting ribs on the grill. The couple laughed and put up their hands in an admission of guilt.

Rachelle smiled at them and turned back toward the house. She froze in her tracks when Pastor and First Lady Taylor opened the gate of the tall wooden fence and entered with their adolescent son.

Please, God, let them be alone.

Did arrow prayers really work? Maybe so, but Rachelle decided hers must be so rusty that an instant answer wasn't guaranteed.

Troy and Chaundra stepped inside the backyard and closed the fence behind them. The girl spotted Indigo and her friends and trotted over to join them. Troy zeroed in on Rachelle and paused.

Her cell phone rang before either of them could react. Thankful for the distraction, she pulled it from the clip attached to her buckle loop and answered without screening the call. It had to be Alanna.

"You won't believe who just showed up," Rachelle said, with her eyes fixed on Troy.

"Really," said a deep voice on the other end that didn't belong to her sister. "Just where are you, anyway?"

Gabe had picked a fine time to call.

11

*G*abe speed dialed Rachelle on his Blackberry five times and each time ended the call before it rang.

He had been gone four days and hadn't heard from his wife. He was so angry he felt like canceling her credit cards. She wouldn't stay gone long with no money.

He wanted to tell her that, but since she was the one with the attitude problem, she should be calling to set things straight. He didn't have time to be tracking her down. Time was money.

But today he couldn't help it. He had to know whether she'd gone back home after she snuck out of the house Wednesday afternoon. He had smashed a glass against a kitchen cabinet when he picked up her voice mail message. If Rachelle hadn't returned and fixed the mess, Helen would wonder what had happened when she arrived to clean the house this week.

Surely, though, Rachelle wasn't going to be stupid. She couldn't be planning to leave for good and give up her lifestyle.

But her complaint about "things" not being enough troubled him. He worked hard, provided well for her and the kids, afforded her nice vacations and entrée into circles of influence most women only fantasized about joining. His work was demanding and sometimes inconvenient, but he made it home for dinner often enough. What else did he have to give? Women could be so needy.

Gabe hadn't called the house all day, assuming he would reach Rachelle on her cell. But maybe she had come to her senses. He tried their home number, and that call went straight to voice mail.

"I know Rachelle is not still at some hotel," he said under his breath and glanced at his watch. He had another session in an hour and would be flying home later that afternoon. Dinner and a massage would be the perfect way to make up.

This time when he dialed her cell number, he didn't hang up. Relief coursed through him when she answered, but it was quickly replaced by anger.

Clearly she had been expecting to hear from someone else. When he asked where she was, she had remained silent long enough for him to fear that she might hang up. He also heard voices in the background.

"Where are you?" he asked again. "Have your hormones settled down yet? Hello?"

"Yes, Gabe, I'm here," she finally responded. "What's with the interrogation?"

"What are you talking about?" he said. "I haven't heard from you since I left Houston. Don't I have a right to know where my wife is? Until the past month, I never had to ask—you made it your job to keep me informed. Why are you tripping all of a sudden?"

Gabe felt his voice rising, along with his blood pressure. He sat in the hotel lounge and tried to appear nonchalant. A pretty doctor he had met at dinner the night before walked past him and waved.

I should have gone to my room for this conversation, he thought. Rachelle wasn't going to cut him any slack.

"Listen to you," she said. "You're right—we haven't talked in four days, and what's the first question you ask me? Are my hormones normal. Then you tell me I'm tripping. That's why I 'tripped' right out the door on Wednesday."

What had gotten into her? Gabe took a deep breath and pressed his lips together to keep from fueling her fire.

"I'm in Jubilant, visiting Aunt Irene and Uncle Charles," she finally said.

Gabe felt sucker-punched. He sat forward in the sofa chair and tried to remain calm as groups of physicians swirled past him. "How long have you been there? Are they having a party or something? When are you coming home?"

The questions flew from his mouth as rapidly as they formed in his mind. Better get them out now before he said something else to anger her.

Lyle Stevens, his surgery partner, stepped off the elevator. He pointed at his watch and Gabe checked the time on his own. Forty minutes until their presentation. Gabe gave him a thumbs-up.

He wasn't getting off the phone with Rachelle, though, until he had some answers.

"I went to San Diego on Friday to visit Jillian and flew into Houston this morning," Rachelle said. "Gabe, she's dying. She had a party to tell her closest friends goodbye."

So that was it. Her childhood and college friend was dying. Now it all made sense. "I'm sorry to hear that, Rachelle," Gabe said. He knew how to handle patients who were struggling with difficult diagnoses. He did it all the time and always received glowing reviews for bedside manner.

"I know this is difficult," he said. "Why didn't you tell me sooner? Why didn't you tell me you were going to California?"

He heard a heavy sigh and suspected she was crying. Gabe

settled back into his seat. "This must be traumatic for you, especially with Jillian being so young. I'm so sorry."

Silence permeated the airwaves.

"You know what, Gabe?"

He could tell that Rachelle was clinching her teeth.

"I am insulted," she said. "I've heard you assume this same tone hundreds of times when you've had to make difficult calls to your patients or their relatives. I would think that you'd have some real empathy to share with your wife, not some canned method you honed in med school."

Gabe winced. He had underestimated her.

"What do you want anyway?" Rachelle asked.

This was it. The moment to get everything back on track. "Look, Rachelle, I'm sorry about everything that I've said or done over the past few days to upset you," Gabe said as softly as he could, hoping that the doctors, who had begun to meet in the lobby for the upcoming sessions, weren't listening. "Just come home so we can figure it out, okay? I'm taking a flight out tonight and will be there by seven p.m. Can you get to Houston by then and pick me up from the airport?"

Rachelle's laugh was short and dry. He wished he could see her face; she sounded so unlike herself.

"Do I have 'Taxi Driver' stamped across my forehead, Gabe? Sorry—can't do it," Rachelle said. "And by the way, I gave Helen the week off, so she's not going to be there, either.

"I'm at Aunt Irene's for a barbecue in honor of Indigo's birthday. She turned fifteen yesterday. Plus, I haven't spent any time with my aunt and uncle in forever, thanks to you. I'm here now, so I might as well stay and enjoy myself."

Gabe rose from the seat and grabbed his briefcase, which sat near his feet. "Rachelle, why are you doing this? I'll be home tonight and I'm leaving for Uganda on Tuesday, remember? What's going on? Are you messing around? Don't be stupid."

Rachelle wasn't the type to cheat, but something clearly had her acting out of character. Did she know about Veronica? He quickly dismissed that thought. He had been too careful.

Maybe it was simply the shock of Jillian's looming death. Whatever the cause, he needed to nip it, because it had Rachelle pushing all the boundaries.

He hated for her to go back to Jubilant without him. Somehow she always wound up on Everson's campus, visiting the special spots she had shared with *Troy* or passing the church where she had eloped with *Troy* or visiting the aunt and uncle who had loved *Troy* as much as they had loved her.

Now she had defied his wishes and was probably there rehashing her past at a time when she was angry with him. At least Troy had moved away a long time ago.

He frowned again and wished he could get her under control. For now, he'd just be happy to have her home.

"Gabe, I'm sorry, but I won't be there tonight," Rachelle said, more calmly this time. "I'll think about coming tomorrow, to be there before you leave for Uganda. In case I don't, I've already packed your bags. They're tucked in the right corner of your closet. Your passport and travel checklist are there too, okay? Be safe."

She ended the call without giving him a chance to respond. Here he was, preparing to travel to Africa, and his wife was abandoning him.

Gabe placed the Blackberry in his belt clip and walked toward Stevens, who was waiting near the elevators, eyeing him.

"Everything all right? Ready for our presentation?"

Gabe forced a smile and clapped his friend and colleague on the back. "Ready as I'll ever be, man. Let's do it."

Right now, work required his focus. Whether it happened tonight or after his ten-day stay in Uganda, he was going to put Rachelle in check. The other docs bragged all the time about straightening out their wives and girlfriends and reminding them who wore the pants. He'd never had a problem with Rachelle, and as far as he was concerned, he wouldn't for much longer.

When he was off of his game because of distractions at home, someone's life potentially could be jeopardized. If she wanted him to continue living up to his duties as her husband, she needed to fall in line as his wife.

12

*R*achelle knew she had gone overboard, but it felt great.

Every jibe she uttered made up for the years of stuffing down her emotions, biting her tongue, and letting Gabe make decisions that weren't always wise or fair.

She hadn't meant to twist the knife, but when he had failed to ask why Jillian was dying or how much longer she might live, Rachelle's hope that he really wanted to make things right faded. The fact that he couldn't muster up genuine concern over the imminent death of a woman she had once been so close to broke her heart.

Granted, Gabe continued to hold a grudge against Jillian for refusing to participate in their wedding; but under these circumstances, none of that mattered.

Rachelle leaned back on Reuben's bed, where she found herself for a second time today fielding a private call. She could hear the partygoers just outside the window, laughing and chatting.

She felt like curling up and taking a nap, which wasn't an option. But then again, facing Troy, who was outside with the other guests, wasn't either.

She sat up and stared at the suitcase in the corner. Technically, she could repeat her actions from a few days ago and sneak out of the house unseen. The thought both intrigued and rattled her.

How would that feel—to up and go, leaving Aunt Irene and Uncle Charles a note, informing them that she would be back to visit at another time? They'd get the message that she didn't appreciate how they had handled Troy's arrival, without her having to initiate another uncomfortable conversation like the one with Uncle Charles this afternoon. And maybe the next time something like this came up, they'd treat her like an adult, instead of a child who needed to be spoon-fed the news.

I should do it, she thought. Her heart pounded as she envisioned the scenario. *Isn't that what I want?*

Well, respect, yes, but not at the risk of losing the adoration she had always received from her aunt and uncle. Was it possible to get both? If she changed the status quo, would their affections shift, too?

Honoring Jillian's request to thrive and be happy wasn't going to be easy. In the few days since she had promised to live in that fashion, she was realizing that she had been existing like a wind-up doll, going through the motions and following expectations set by others. She had somehow numbed herself to the possibility of writing her own script, like Jillian had managed to do.

Was it too late? She just didn't know. But hurting Aunt Irene's and Uncle Charles's feelings this afternoon wasn't the answer. Jillian hadn't told her to rush the process; she had simply urged her to begin.

Rachelle surveyed Reuben's walls, which were plastered with an eclectic mix of posters, ranging from those featuring the poses of his favorite sports figures to the beguiling glances of singers Beyoncé and Rihanna.

She chuckled. Is this what she had to look forward to when Tate was older?

She stood up and stretched. She didn't want to, but she knew she had to return to the barbecue before Aunt Irene or Aunt Melba came searching for her. She had to face Troy Hardy.

Rachelle followed the hallway from the bedroom to the kitchen, as before. This time the pictures didn't distract her; she was trying to prepare for whatever awaited her outside.

However, just as she reached for the double-paned door leading to the backyard, Troy pulled it open. The two of them nearly collided. He kept her from tripping over his feet by grabbing her arm.

Great, Rachelle thought, *just great*.

Troy quickly let go once she had steadied herself.

"Hello, Rachelle," he said. "Sorry about that. I'm looking for the bathroom."

He stepped aside and pulled the door open so she could exit.

She was surprised, expecting him to try and make small talk.

"Thanks, Troy. It's right down the hallway." She motioned to the area she'd just left, but made no effort to walk past him. "It's nice to see you. Congratulations on your position at the church. I didn't know you were pursuing music as a career."

She could have kicked herself. That sounded so dumb. How would she know what he had been doing for the past decade unless she had been stalking him?

Her eyes were drawn to his dimpled chin when he smiled at her. He was about ten pounds heavier, but it was in all the right places. She thought about her hastily secured ponytail and her rumpled, sweaty outfit. She must look a hot mess.

"Yep, I've been fortunate to use both sides of my brain—the artistic and analytical sides," Troy said. "Engineering and music have been a good combination."

He was still holding the door open for her and gave her a quizzical look. Rachelle had more questions—like where was the mother of his child?—but didn't want to seem overly interested.

Humph. Funny how the tables had turned. She had been intent on fleeing from him after church today, but he didn't seem the least bit fazed by her.

She nodded and stepped outside. "Well, good to see you. I hope you and your daughter enjoy St. Peter's."

Troy hesitated and cleared his throat. "I'm sure we will. Pastor Taylor is a great leader, and the members have already given us a warm welcome. It's good to see you, Rachelle."

With that, he slid into the kitchen and let the door close behind him.

Rachelle stood there for a moment to get her bearings. The encounter had been odd. Not as uncomfortable as she had expected, but somehow unsettling for that very reason.

She shook her head to clear her thoughts and wandered over to the grill, where Aunt Melba was begging Uncle Charles to burn her a hot dog.

"You know how I like them—nice and crispy," Melba said.

Uncle Charles shook his head. "You and your burnt stuff, girl. Burnt baloney, burnt hot dogs, burnt—"

"Dates!" Melba finished for him and laughed.

"Dates?" Rachelle asked and laughed. "Are you still breaking hearts, Aunt Melba?"

She smiled slyly. "Can't tell all my business, niecey. Some things need to remain between me and the Lord. I'm single, so I can keep looking."

She put her hand on her hip and leveled her eyes at Rachelle. "You on the other hand? Watch it. I just saw that exchange with Mr. Ex-Husband in the doorway. Be careful, Rachelle."

13

By the time the last guest left around nine p.m., Rachelle was emotionally and physically spent.

Jet lag from her early morning flight had caught up with her, and she struggled to make small talk with Aunt Irene and Uncle Charles while they tidied the kitchen.

Everyone in the Burns family, except the resident teenager, seemed ready to fall into bed too. Indigo had wandered off to the family room with her cell phone attached to her ear, chattering with the same level of energy she possessed six hours earlier.

Rachelle returned to Reuben's bedroom and removed her sandals. This time she lay across his twin-sized bed as if she owned it.

She hadn't slept in something this small in forever, but if Reuben, who was nearly six feet, could fit comfortably, she figured she should fit too. At least the mattress was firm.

There was a light rap on the door and Aunt Irene peeked inside. "Got a minute to chat, or are you about to pass out?"

Rachelle rubbed her eyes and sat up. "Come in, Aunt Irene; we haven't had a chance to catch up. Besides, I need to talk to Tate and Taryn before I call it a night."

Aunt Irene shuffled into the room and eased herself onto the bed.

"When will you have your hip replacement surgery?" Rachelle asked.

Aunt Irene sighed. "Soon, I hope. My doctor was scheduled to perform it last month, but had a ministroke. Another orthopedic surgeon has taken on Dr. Cain's patients in addition to his own, so he hasn't let me know yet when he can work me in."

Rachelle patted her hand. "It seems painful . . . Is that why you had something stronger than water in that red cup?"

A wave of embarrassment crossed Aunt Irene's face. "I was joking with you. You know me better than that!"

Rachelle wasn't convinced, but didn't press the issue. She had no right to interrogate her aunt.

"Enough about me. What's going on with you?" Aunt Irene asked. "Why are you here without Gabe? And why did you run inside at the first sighting of Troy? He's not going to bite, you know. I know it's uncomfortable, but it's reality."

"If it's reality, then why didn't you tell me that he had been hired by your church?" Rachelle bit her tongue. "Sorry."

Aunt Irene ignored Rachelle's tone and her apology. "Again, I'm asking, what's going on?"

Rachelle shrugged. "I don't know. I'm just fed up. I don't know what I want anymore and whether I even want to be with Gabe anymore. I'm tired of being with someone who thinks the world revolves around him and that as his wife, I'm here to cater to him."

Aunt Irene leveled her gaze at Rachelle. "Let's get real, young lady. The man you're describing is the same man you met soon after moving to Houston for optometry school. He was self-absorbed then and he's self-absorbed now. I know you didn't marry him expecting to change him. Did you?"

Rachelle sat back and looked at her aunt. "What do you mean Gabe was self-absorbed? I thought you liked him. I mean I know you weren't crazy about him like you were about . . .Troy, but still."

Aunt Irene shook her head. "Rachelle, this has nothing to do with me liking or disliking Gabe. That should only matter for you—you're the one who has to live with him.

"But in response to your comment, I never knew him as well as Troy, because you two began dating after you graduated from Everson. However, I saw what I saw, and I thought you did too. Didn't I tell you before you married him to expect the things you liked about him to get better and the things that annoyed you to get worse?

"I know I must have," Aunt Irene said, "because it's true. When you're in love, you see everything through those rose-colored glasses. The things that get on your nerves are okay because he's your prince, or in Gabe's case, your king. But let a few years pass and get a few babies and a few bills, and those same things can drive you right out the door."

Rachelle pursed her lips. "What if I really didn't love him? What if I just thought I did? Or, I was taking my chance with him because I kept hearing he was a 'good catch,' and I didn't want to be old and lonely?"

Aunt Irene smiled. "As pretty as you are, that should have never entered your mind," she said. "But you wouldn't be the first to choose a mate for that reason. That doesn't always mean you won't grow into love, but it can make for a harder road to travel.

"Now, here you are, deep into this, with two kids to think about and, what? Are you thinking of leaving him?"

Rachelle shrugged and lowered her head. "I kinda have," she said. "He's coming home from a medical conference tonight and I'm here. He leaves for Uganda on Tuesday, and I don't think I'm going home to see him off."

She lifted her eyes to gauge Aunt Irene's reaction. There was none.

"Can you believe Gabe is even going on a medical mission trip?" Rachelle continued. "It's Christian-based too. The church that his surgery partner attends is heavily involved, and Lyle finally convinced him to go along."

Aunt Irene nodded. "See what I mean? Do you hear yourself? Even what you're saying about him now makes him sound like he's more into himself than anyone else—you're surprised that he would go on a mission trip, to help others in need," she said. "What you're going to have to decide is how you can be the Rachelle God has called you to be, regardless of what Gabe wants or demands from you, because in the end, you'll have to stand before him one day for yourself, and be accountable for how you used this life he gave you.

"But"—Aunt Irene raised a forefinger—"I'm not saying that you can't do that and stay with your husband. Marriage is a ministry too, you know. God can work through a union centered on him to do wonderful things that bless others."

Rachelle frowned. "A ministry? Okay, that's a new one for me."

Aunt Irene laughed. "Trust me. If I didn't believe that the life Charles and I have created together somehow draws others to God, and if I didn't understand that one of my reasons for staying committed is to honor my promise before God, I might have left a few times myself."

Rachelle's dismay must have registered on her face.

"That's okay," Aunt Irene said. "I know you're thinking that your favorite uncle couldn't possibly have done anything wrong. He is a good man, Rachelle, but he's still a man. And no matter how good he is, unless you have to live with him, you just don't know!

"But back to you. You have to find Rachelle's purpose, and use that to guide you toward happiness and fulfillment."

Rachelle thought again about her blank Top Ten List. "That's the second time in less than a week that I've received advice like that. You remember my friend Jillian?"

Aunt Irene smiled. "Yes! How is that lovely girl doing? She had a bright future when she graduated from Everson. I just knew she was going to do well."

Rachelle smiled. "She has done well, Aunt Irene. She continued with her photography and has traveled the world shooting pictures for *National Geographic* magazine. And you know what? Somewhere along the way, she found God."

Aunt Irene raised an eyebrow. "Did she, now? Actually, Rachelle, God was there all along. Jillian must have decided 'somewhere along the way' to open her heart to him."

Rachelle pondered that perspective. Was that why she couldn't hear from God—because her heart wasn't open?

"I saw Jillian over the weekend for the first time in years," Rachelle said. "You probably remember that she didn't come to my wedding, and after that we fell out of touch. Now she's dying, Aunt Irene. She has breast cancer."

Aunt Irene clutched her chest. "Jillian?"

Rachelle nodded. "She has been given only a few weeks to live. I don't know what process she went through, but she seems to be at peace."

Rachelle told Aunt Irene about the party Jillian hosted. Aunt

Irene hugged her and held her. Rachelle's defenses crumbled. She wept into her aunt's shoulder.

When she finally lifted her head, Rachelle was embarrassed. "Guess you got more than you bargained for when you came in here, huh?"

Aunt Irene shook her head. "You're fine," she said. "And trust me, there will be more days when the tears overwhelm you. Losing someone who was special to you is hard; it's just plain hard. I understand now why you're feeling confused about everything."

"A lot is happening," Rachelle said.

"That is a lot," Aunt Irene said. "And then you show up here, hoping to get away from it all, and discover that Troy has returned."

Rachelle nodded as a fresh round of tears filled her eyes. "I can't believe I still get upset about what happened back then. My parents altered my entire future. I could have been up there today with Troy, being welcomed back to Jubilant."

Aunt Irene frowned. "Now don't go getting ahead of yourself. You don't know how life would have unfolded if the two of you had stayed together. It's easy to speculate the best of circumstances when you don't know what the day-to-day reality would have been like."

Rachelle looked into Aunt Irene's eyes. "Yes, but Troy loved me. I made a mistake. I should have chosen to honor my marriage vows and refused to leave him. Instead, I listened to Mom and Dad's threats and chose a career over my husband. I practiced optometry all of two years before Gabe insisted that I quit and be more available to him and little Tate, so what was the point?"

"There's always a point, Rachelle," Aunt Irene said. "Always.

The key is to figure out how God can effectively use you where you're planted now, regardless of how you got there."

Rachelle averted her eyes. Since she was being honest, she might as well tell it all. "That's just it, Aunt Irene," she said. "This God thing? It isn't working for me. He hasn't found me, he doesn't speak to me, and I don't anticipate him dropping a note about my purpose in my email inbox anytime soon. I hear what you're saying, and it all sounds wonderful—Jillian mentioned some of the same things during her party. But how can what you're saying help me? I don't know the last time I had a connection with 'the Man upstairs.'"

Aunt Irene smiled and slowly lifted herself off the bed. "You need to find your way to him, Rachelle. He's there, in the circumstances already around you, waiting to embrace you and guide you."

She crept toward the door, but kept talking. "The question is, do you want to be 'found'? Do you want answers to all of these questions you have? Sometimes people think they do, but they'd rather stay in the dark."

Aunt Irene grabbed the doorknob. Before she departed, she turned and looked at Rachelle. "Trust me, that's way more comfortable. I haven't always known the Lord like I do now. And even now, I mess up. But think about Jillian: Everything isn't perfect, yet she knows where she's headed. That's a beautiful thing. Look at Troy. Isn't it amazing how God has brought him full circle and sent him back to the place he once called home?"

Rachelle attempted to smile. She didn't want to be rude, but in some ways, Aunt Irene's faith sounded like mindless devotion. Her scientific-minded friends in Houston often watched the Bible-belt televangelists and ridiculed viewers who sent in love offerings to support the ministers' lavish churches and lifestyles. Rachelle had also found them amusing.

Tonight, however, Aunt Irene had given her a glimpse of how faith could be relevant. Still, Rachelle wanted to know why, if God was so good, Aunt Irene had needed whatever she was drinking earlier today.

14

The timid knock at the door startled Rachelle. She sat up in bed and tried to get her bearings.

It took her a few seconds to realize that she didn't recognize her surroundings because they weren't hers. Reuben's bed was comfortable. She had been in a deep sleep.

The light tapping at the door continued.

"Good morning! Yes?" she said.

"Cousin Rachelle, I have a hair appointment but Mama doesn't feel well this morning and she's still in bed. Can you please take me to Aunt Melba's salon?"

Indigo sounded desperate.

Rachelle glanced at the clock again. Of course she couldn't tell the child no. She rose from the bed and pulled her robe from her suitcase.

She opened the door and smiled at the ninth grader, who had inherited her father's lanky frame and broad smile. Indigo's hair had been combed into a frizzy ponytail, the remnants of the water balloon fight she and her friends had at yesterday's birthday barbecue.

"Sure. What time do you have to be there?" Rachelle asked.

They agreed to get dressed and meet in the kitchen in thirty minutes. Rachelle rummaged through her bag, still filled with her clothing from San Diego, and found the pair of jeans she had packed. She pulled out a gold camisole and the honey brown ballet flats she had worn for her trek through the airport.

After a quick shower, she strolled into the kitchen fully dressed and ready to go. Uncle Charles was flipping pancakes while Indigo and Yasmin sat at the table, waiting to be served. Indigo was listening to her purple iPod and reading a novel while Yasmin played with her pink handheld electronic game. Rachelle stifled a laugh. These could be her children, who also had traded in their Game Boys a couple of years ago for the next new gadgets.

Rachelle waved at them and Indigo set aside her distractions.

"Good morning, family," Rachelle said. She remembered waking up to Uncle Charles's feasts during her days at Everson College, whenever she visited during the weekend. He always had breakfast duty and Aunt Irene prepared the rest of the meals.

"I see you're still a pro in the kitchen," Rachelle told him. She pulled out a chair and joined the girls at the rectangular oak table.

"He just does this to impress our guests," Indigo said. "We don't get this kind of service on a regular basis. So please, come more often."

Uncle Charles placed dishes filled with warm scrambled eggs and slices of bacon in the center of the table. He slid plates stacked with pancakes in front of Rachelle and his daughters.

On his way back to the stove, he thumped the side of Indigo's head with his thumb and forefinger.

"Hey!" she protested.

Rachelle laughed at their playful exchange. Sadness flickered in her heart for a second when she considered how Gabe never interacted like that with Taryn, and neither had her dad with her.

Uncle Charles flipped another set of pancakes. They were perfectly round and golden. He gave himself a thumbs-up.

"Thanks for taking Indigo to Melba's," he said as he moved about. "I took the day off from the car dealership since not too many people buy on Mondays during the summer. I'm going to remove those tents from yesterday's barbecue and catch up on some projects around the house. Your Aunt Irene went to bed last night with a splitting headache. She's still sleeping."

Rachelle remembered the cup Aunt Irene had clutched most of yesterday, even while they sang "Happy Birthday" to Indigo. She wondered if Uncle Charles knew the likely cause of Aunt Irene's ailment.

She was puzzled by the contrast between the thoughtful conversation she and Aunt Irene had just last night and what she was hearing now. Other than her sore hips, Aunt Irene had seemed coherent.

Uncle Charles placed the last pancake onto a clean plate and held it out to Indigo. "Take this to your Mama."

Indigo focused her attention on the last bite of her eggs and bacon, without responding. Uncle Charles set the plate on the table, in front of her.

"Did you hear me?" he asked.

Rachelle couldn't ever recall seeing him angry. If Indigo was like every other teenager Rachelle knew, the girl would be mortified that her father was yelling at her in front of company. Rachelle rose from the table and headed down the hall to give them some privacy.

"I'll get my purse and meet you at the car, Indigo," she said.

Rachelle entered Reuben's bedroom and leaned against the back of the door. What was going on with the Burns family? Maybe having an adolescent girl was testing Uncle Charles's mettle.

Rachelle grabbed her bag and trotted back down the hallway. She peered into the kitchen and saw Uncle Charles was standing near Indigo, whispering heatedly. The girl's face was expressionless.

If she's anything like I was at that age, she is furious, Rachelle thought.

She trusted Uncle Charles's child rearing judgment, but she empathized with Indigo. Sometimes parents didn't get it; they put you in a box with a label affixed and tried to keep you there forever.

Rather than interrupt them, Rachelle decided to leave through the front door. Her car was parked out front anyway. She had moved it to the street before yesterday's cookout so that Aunt Irene and Uncle Charles's older guests wouldn't have to walk far.

The heat engulfed Rachelle when she stepped outside onto the porch. Yasmin sat on the stoop, waiting for her. She looked up and offered Rachelle a puppy dog smile.

"Cousin Rachelle, will you please take me over to my friend Carmen's house to play? Daddy called her mama, and she said it was okay. There's nothing going on around this boring house."

Indigo, who had followed Rachelle outside, smirked. "You're seven," she told Yasmin. "Play with your dolls and be happy."

Yasmin clearly was used to her older sister's disdain. She waited for Rachelle's response, and when Rachelle nodded, she trotted off to find a few treasures to take with her. "Gimme just a minute, okay?"

Yasmin returned with a pink backpack stuffed with who knows what. Rachelle recognized one of the lumps as a doll, but didn't ask what else was enclosed.

Indigo rolled her eyes. "You spend more time over there with your little friend than you do at home."

Rachelle glanced at Indigo to gauge if the girl was serious, but couldn't decide. That didn't sound like something Aunt Irene would approve of, but then again, quite a few things seemed out of sorts. Whether they were worthy of concern was up for debate. Rachelle hoped she was reading more into things than she should.

15

*R*achelle pulled away from the curb and followed Yasmin's directions to Carmen's house, two blocks away. Twenty minutes later, she and Indigo turned into the parking lot adjacent to Hair Pizzazz, Aunt Melba's salon. The squat, red-brick building that housed the business didn't fit Aunt Melba's stylish image. When clients entered, however, they often referred to the atmosphere as a chic or elegant haven.

Rachelle noticed that Aunt Melba had changed the décor since she had last ventured to the salon several years ago. The jewel-tone color scheme had been replaced by faux-finished, muted gold walls. Two sofas in the waiting area had been reupholstered in a Tuscany red, and an Oriental rug that covered most of the open floor emphasized both colors.

Live ferns were strategically placed on pedestals near each window and eclectic paintings graced the walls. It appeared that Aunt Melba still offered art majors from Everson College opportunities to display their work.

The soft jazz pouring through the speakers soothed Rachelle's ears. She wasn't getting her hair done today, but she had a feeling she'd leave here relaxed, just the same.

Other than Indigo, Aunt Melba had only two clients this

morning, and one of them was Dr. Cynthia Bridgeforth. She waved to Rachelle and Indigo from under the dryer.

Aunt Melba motioned for Indigo to sit in her chair. She draped a black cape over the girl and fastened it at the neck while Rachelle stood with her and watched.

"I love the new décor, Aunt Melba." Rachelle glanced around, admiring the makeover again. "When did you do all of this?"

"About six months ago," Melba said. "It's good to change things up every so often, you know? If I've got to be in here ten or twelve hours a day for most of the week, it's like a second home, and I need to love it."

Rachelle smiled. "Well, I love it too. Jubilant, Texas, isn't going to be able to handle you in a minute. This is classy."

Aunt Melba paused and put her hand on her hip. "Watch it now. Don't be talking about my town. Jubilant isn't Houston, but we aren't all hicks, Miss Thang. You fit in right nicely before you became 'Mrs. Cardiac Surgeon America.'"

They both laughed.

"Do you always come in on Mondays?" Rachelle asked, purposely changing the subject. She would rather focus on her independent, feisty aunt this morning than on her own trophy-wife woes. "I thought most hairstylists took this day off."

Aunt Melba nodded. "I'm usually closed, but I couldn't fit Cynthia in on Saturday, and she has an important function tonight. Then Indigo had so much fun at her party yesterday that she got her hair all wet and jacked it up."

The three of them laughed. Melba motioned toward an older woman sitting under a dryer next to Cynthia.

"And Lela Cooley over there? She's recovering from cancer and her hair is finally growing back. She called me on Saturday and told me she thought that enough had returned for her to throw away her wig and start getting it styled again. Since I was booked up and couldn't squeeze her in, I told her to come today.

"I'll have all of these folks in and out of my chair by one p.m.," Aunt Melba said. "Got one more young lady coming in after Indigo, and the rest of the day will be mine."

Aunt Melba walked Indigo to the shampoo bowl and wet and lathered the girl's hair. Rachelle took a seat in the chair Indigo had vacated and watched.

When Aunt Melba had washed and rinsed twice, she slathered on conditioner and slid on a plastic cap. She instructed Indigo to close her eyes and relax for a few minutes.

Melba dried her hands with the white towel she kept on the rack behind the sink, then motioned for Rachelle to follow her through a door, into the salon's supply room.

"What's up, Aunt Melba?" Rachelle asked.

In her camel halter top, matching jeans, and wedge sandals, Melba looked ready for a casual chic photo shoot. She folded her arms and pursed her lips.

"You tell me," she said. "What are you doing down here, hanging around town just when your ex-husband happens to move back and your current husband is nowhere to be found? You're playing with fire, Rachelle."

Rachelle frowned. "Aunt Melba," she said slowly, grasping for a response she wouldn't later regret. "I'm not sure what you're thinking, but I'm not up to anything. I came to visit yesterday and didn't realize that Troy was here, or that St. Peter's Baptist had hired him. No idea. I wouldn't have shown up if that were the case. And when I saw him at the barbecue yesterday, I almost grabbed my suitcase and drove home.

"I'm not playing games," Rachelle continued. "I'm a grown woman and I'm married to someone else."

Melba stared at her. "So you didn't know he would be bringing Chaundra in this morning to get her hair done?"

Rachelle caught her breath. Another encounter? "Troy is coming here? I'll leave and come back to pick up Indigo when you're done."

Melba wasn't fazed by Rachelle's frustration. "If it's no big deal, why do you need to disappear every time he's around?" she asked. "I don't go to church often, but I was there yesterday, sitting on one of the last rows, and I saw you flee after service. I also saw you dash inside with your cell phone when he arrived at the barbecue."

Rachelle was busted. She had been running, as if not sharing the same space with Troy would limit her exposure to her previous heartbreak. Then, when she had finally talked with him, she was the one who hadn't wanted the conversation to end.

Even so, Rachelle wasn't sure why Aunt Melba was pushing her so hard.

"It's not so cut-and-dried," Rachelle said. "We were more than just college sweethearts, Aunt Melba. I eloped with him. It's an awkward situation. But why are you so up in arms about this?"

Aunt Melba paused for the longest time, clearly debating whether to answer. "I'm just looking out for you, Rachelle. I don't know what's going on with you and Gabe, but I don't think you should let this encounter with Troy blur your reason. God has a purpose for everything and everyone, including you."

Rachelle's eyes widened. Aunt Melba was the life of the party, not the spiritual sage. Where was this coming from?

"Don't look so surprised!" Aunt Melba said. "God can work through anybody!"

They both chuckled.

"Look," Aunt Melba said. "If you need to talk anything through,

I'm here. I just see the potential for problems and I want you to make sure you keep your guard up."

Rachelle gave her a light hug. "Thanks for caring, Auntie, but no need to worry," she said. "Besides, Troy didn't have two cents' worth of time or words for me yesterday. He has moved on."

The women returned to the salon's studio. Indigo still rested at the sink with her eyes closed while Cynthia sat at a dryer with the hood up, waiting to have her hair combed and styled. Melba's other client, Lela, had dozed off under the dryer.

Rachelle sauntered over to Cynthia and greeted her with a hug. Before long, Rachelle was quizzing the pediatrician about her work.

"It can be grueling, but I enjoy what I do," Cynthia said. "I easily see fifteen to twenty patients a day, and they usually have a long wait, because I take the time to talk with the mothers about everything that's going on in their families, not just about their child's growth and development.

"A lot of my parents are just teenagers themselves, so their lives are challenging," Cynthia said. "I realized a long time ago that God didn't allow me to become a doctor just to administer medical advice. This is my social ministry."

"That is so meaningful," Rachelle said. "Not that providing pediatric services alone isn't. But to offer everything else that you're doing for your patients—wow. Most doctors aren't giving patients books or making sure they get screened onsite for asthma and diabetes."

Cynthia shrugged. "I grew up in a single parent home where my mother stressed education and excellence. If not for that, I wouldn't have dreamt of becoming a doctor. I might have been one of those teenage mothers I now help, if not for her. That's why I do it."

She shifted in her seat. "Now, you know more about my work than you ever wanted to," she said and laughed. "Tell me your story, Rachelle. Melba told me you're an optometrist?"

Rachelle was surprised her aunt had thought to mention the career she hadn't pursued in so long. "Aunt Melba remembers that? Yes, I'm a trained optometrist, but I haven't practiced in years. I stopped soon after my ten-year-old son was born." She hesitated, then lowered her voice. "Few people know this, but I renew my license every year, even though I'm not working in the field. Is that silly or what?"

Cynthia shook her head and smiled. "I'm a firm believer that few things are coincidental. You've been renewing that license for a reason. Time will tell you what it's for."

A bell chimed when the salon door swung open. Troy ushered in Chaundra, who grinned when she saw Indigo sitting at the shampoo bowl.

Troy waved at Melba. "Hello, ladies," he said to Rachelle and Cynthia. His eyes swept past the empty chairs on either side of them, near the dryers, and the vacant sofas in the waiting area.

Rachelle knew he was weighing his options. She picked up a magazine from the seat next to her and zoned in on actress Gabrielle Union's face.

Cynthia motioned to the seat next to her. Troy shrugged and slid into it.

"I'm not getting my hair washed and dried, but I guess I can sit here," he joked and ran his hand over his smooth, fair-skinned head.

The three sat in silence, watching Melba work. Indigo had asked Aunt Melba to turn on the radio, and India.Arie's smooth alto was now piping through the speakers.

"It's about forgiveness . . . even if, even if you don't love me anymore . . ."

Perfect, Rachelle thought. She and Aunt Melba locked eyes.

"You guys can turn to another station or put in a CD, if you'd like," Aunt Melba said.

No one moved.

She combed through Indigo's wet hair and positioned her under the dryer next to Rachelle. She motioned for Cynthia to have a seat in her chair, so she could begin styling her hair.

That left Troy and Rachelle sitting two seats apart, staring anywhere but at each other.

"Want to move to the waiting area?" Troy finally said. "I won't bite, you know."

Rachelle looked at him and tried to control her emotions. She couldn't believe after all this time that some of the pain, and a lot of the desire, lingered.

When she didn't respond, he picked up a magazine and strolled over to one of the red sofas.

Rachelle stayed put and kept her magazine on page sixty-five for the next hour, staring at the featured words and images, but really not seeing them. She wasn't sure why she was so uncomfortable, but wished it weren't so obvious.

No wonder Aunt Melba felt the need to lecture her. She had to get herself together. Troy had moved on and so had she—at least on the surface. No one needed to know differently.

When Indigo was ready, with her freshly washed hair hanging just below her ears in a stylish, asymmetrical cut, Rachelle stood up and grabbed her purse.

"That is beautiful, Aunt Melba. I'm going to have to get Taryn down here," she said.

Indigo and Chaundra exchanged phone numbers and made

plans to talk later that day. Indigo trotted over to Troy, in the waiting area.

"Can Chaundra come over and hang out sometime, Mr. Hardy?"

He looked at Rachelle, then returned his attention to Indigo. "You girls let me know when."

Rachelle surmised what he was thinking. He knew the Burns family well enough to know that if Chaundra and Indigo became friends, she would be keeping good company.

He opened his magazine again and seemed engrossed in whatever he was reading. Rachelle took a deep breath and paused as she passed him on her way out of the salon.

"Take care, Troy," she said. "I'll be leaving for Houston in the next day or so. It was good to see you, and to meet your daughter."

He responded without raising his head. "It was nice to see you too, Rachelle," he said. "Have a safe trip home. And by the way, I don't have children. Chaundra is my niece."

16

Why was Troy raising someone else's teenager? How had he wound up caring for a niece?

The questions ricocheted through Rachelle's mind while she drove to a local hamburger joint to grab lunch with Indigo. The girl was chattering about something, but Rachelle was lost in her thoughts.

She had met Troy's mother and two siblings soon after they began dating during her sophomore year at Everson. Troy invited her to join the family whenever they visited him on campus.

After they eloped, he had taken her to his mother's modest home in Dallas for the first time, so they could share their news. Ms. Hardy was disappointed that they hadn't waited, but she had given her blessing when they promised to graduate as scheduled in six months and go on to grad school.

Troy's brother, Terrance, was teaching middle school in a Dallas suburb and had recently married his college sweetheart. His sister, Tania, had just begun high school and was an academic scholar and cheerleader, headed for the same success as her brothers. How had he wound up with custody of one of their kids?

That question led to another burning one: if he could take care of someone else's child, why didn't he have a wife and family of his own, as fine and accomplished as he was? Something didn't add up.

Maybe I did the right thing by leaving . . .

The rush of relief Rachelle felt behind that knee-jerk sentiment was short-lived. She knew the next time she saw Troy, she'd still be squirming and struggling to ignore the heart palpitations she experienced whenever she was in his presence. And at least he seemed to have an agenda for his life.

A shrill siren pulled her back to reality. She steered the Lexus to the right, even though an ambulance was speeding in the opposite direction.

Seconds later, she pulled back into traffic and turned onto the busy street that led to Fat Joe's Burgers. They wouldn't be eating there today, she realized. Thompson Avenue was blocked.

Several wrecked cars were splayed across the road, and at least four police vehicles, with blue lights flashing, surrounded them. Another ambulance was leaving the scene at a slower pace, without the blasting siren, and a tow truck driver was trying to properly position his vehicle in front of one of the cars.

Indigo had taken her iPod from her purse when she realized Rachelle wasn't listening to her and had become engrossed in a music video unfolding on the media player's screen. She raised her head when the stalled traffic forced Rachelle to reduce her speed. They sat in a line of cars making U-turns under a police officer's direction.

"This is a big accident for the middle of the day," Rachelle said.

Rachelle inched forward and was preparing to turn around when Indigo did a double-take. The girl lowered the window on the passenger door and leaned out to get a better view of the accident.

"Cousin Rachelle! Stop!"

Rachelle smashed on the brakes. The car jerked to a halt. "What?"

Indigo pointed and began to cry. "That's Mama's car! In the middle of the street! All bent up! I don't see her anywhere!"

Rachelle looked through the window, past the officer who was striding toward her with a frown. Indigo was right. The vehicle being lifted onto the tow truck resembled Aunt Irene's navy Cadillac DeVille.

Rachelle was about to pull ahead, into a doughnut shop parking lot, when the officer reached the car and leaned inside the passenger window.

"Is there a problem? We need to keep it moving, ma'am," he said.

"Sir, I believe that's my aunt's car," Rachelle said and pointed toward the Cadillac, which was now resting on the bed of the tow truck. "Is she okay? Was she taken to the hospital in one of those ambulances?"

The officer gave her a once-over. He glanced at Indigo, who was sobbing. "Pull over to that lot," he said, indicating the area Rachelle had been headed toward anyway. He yelled to another officer to take over directing the traffic and approached Rachelle's car.

Before the policeman could reach them, she and Indigo unbuckled themselves and jumped out of their seats. He picked up his pace when he realized they were about to walk toward the accident scene.

"You two ladies, hold it," he said.

Rachelle paused, but Indigo kept going. Mr. Keystone Cop needed to chill.

She saw fear in Indigo's eyes and her heart went out to the girl. She must be about to flip out.

"My cousin needs to make sure her mother is alright, okay?" Rachelle said. "Can you tell me if Irene Burns was driving that car?"

The officer didn't bend. "We're only authorized to release information to next of kin, to the person an accident victim instructs us to call."

Rachelle wanted to yell at him and tell him to look at the terror in Indigo's eyes and forget the rules. She wanted to shake him into humanity.

She took a deep breath instead and tried to calm herself before she made things worse. Plus, it sounded as if Aunt Irene, or whoever the accident victims were, had felt up to talking. That was good.

Indigo trotted back to Rachelle's side.

"What happened?" she asked the policeman, still whimpering.

He hesitated, then looked into her eyes. "Someone was drinking and driving, little lady. That person caused an accident and two people were injured and sent to the hospital."

Indigo's face fell. "One of the drivers was drinking? Was it my mother?"

Rachelle frowned at the officer. She wasn't sure she wanted him to answer. "Have you notified the people the victims asked you to call? Was one of them Charles Burns? If so, he's my uncle."

The officer looked at the two of them and sighed. "Give me a minute."

He walked toward the accident scene and approached an officer who was holding a clipboard and taking notes. Rachelle watched them as they chatted. The traffic officer headed back toward them, but gave no hint of what he had discovered.

"Charles Burns is one of the people we contacted," the officer told Rachelle. "Apparently he is on his way to meet the victim at the hospital."

"I knew it was my mama!" Indigo started to weep again.

The officer approached her and touched her shoulder. "I think she's gonna be fine, little lady. Her hip was bothering her more than anything. The emergency crew transported her to Jubilant Memorial in the ambulance because she wasn't able to stand up without a lot of pain. The car is being towed to a lot on Main Street and will be there until she's ready to reclaim it."

Rachelle thanked him and grabbed Indigo's hand. She led the girl back to the car and once settled, headed in the direction of Jubilant's only hospital.

"What's your dad's cell phone number?"

Indigo rattled off the digits in two seconds. When Rachelle reached a red light, she dialed it quickly. *Please let him answer,* she prayed. Indigo couldn't keep it together much longer.

Uncle Charles picked up on the third ring.

"We just left the scene of the accident," Rachelle said before he could greet her. "Are you at the hospital? Any word yet?"

"I'm a few minutes away, Rachelle," Uncle Charles said. "Sounds like she may have broken her hip, but we won't know until they take X-rays. She's in a lot of pain."

Rachelle looked over at Indigo, who was waiting for answers. "It's okay, Indie. Your mom is hurt, but she doesn't have life-threatening injuries. Your dad's almost at the hospital."

Rachelle knew that limited information was little consolation for her cousin.

"Did they tell you what happened?" she asked Uncle Charles.

His silence was worrisome. "I was told that drinking might have been involved, but I don't have any details yet," he finally said.

"We'll see you in a few minutes," Rachelle said softly. She ended the call and kept her eyes on the road.

Whatever the cause of the accident, and regardless of who was at fault, the Burns family had revisited painful territory. All of their lives had been altered by a previous car accident years ago. The only positive today was that instead of a tragedy, this time it was just a close call.

17

Gabe wandered through his mansion one more time and made his way upstairs, where he kicked the bedroom door shut.

With the kids gone and Rachelle nowhere to be found, the house felt more like a museum than a home. He strolled over to the sitting area and stretched out on the chaise, knowing it wasn't a wise move. When he was idle, his mind traveled in too many directions.

Right now, he wanted to know what Rachelle was doing. Was she spending all of her time with her aunt and uncle? Had they taken her to church? Was she visiting her former professors on campus and fielding questions about her first and second marriages?

Gabe was confident that anything she said about him would wow people. Who wasn't impressed with a heart surgeon?

But where was Troy these days, and did Rachelle still have feelings for him? Gabe was more than curious, especially with the way she had been acting lately.

True to her word, however, she had packed his bags for Uganda before she left. He wanted to call and thank her, but then again, he wanted her to reach out to him. She was punishing him, and it wasn't right.

The phone rang and Gabe leapt to check caller ID. Instead of it being Rachelle, it was his surgical partner, Lyle Stevens. He tried to mask his disappointment.

"Hey man, what's up?" Stevens asked.

He was the coolest white guy Gabe knew. Gray had overtaken his blonde hair, but Lyle Stevens exercised faithfully and was in top shape, and he still carried himself with the confidence of a man who knew his rugged good looks and piercing blue eyes caused women to swoon.

Most of them didn't care so much about his intelligence, but Gabe appreciated that Stevens was also the smartest guy he knew. They had practiced together for six years and, at one point, had joked about understanding each other better than either of them understood their spouses.

That fact had once been a bragging point at parties, and until recently, Gabe hadn't realized that it might have bothered Rachelle. She never let on.

Stevens did an about-face four years ago. He and his wife, Chrissa, left their stoic, traditional congregation for a nondenominational church that emphasized daily Bible study as central to forming a deeper relationship with Christ. To Gabe, it had sounded strange, and even cultish, but the longer Stevens attended, the healthier and happier he seemed.

He and Chrissa eventually had determined, through prayer and discussions with church leaders, that their life's purpose included using their practical skills and sharing their faith with people in Africa and other Third World countries. For the past three years, they had traveled to Uganda to provide medical care and lead Bible studies in the small towns surrounding Kampala, the nation's capital. They lavished most of their attention on an orphanage run by a Ugandan minister and his wife, where children who called the place home thrived.

This year, Stevens had recruited both Gabe and Veronica Hayes, one of the nurses who assisted them during surgeries, to make the trip. They would join Stevens and his wife and five others from the church, and each of them had assigned tasks. While Gabe, Stevens, and another doctor on the team would treat patients in local hospitals and villages, Chrissa and the others would distribute special mosquito nets that helped prevent malaria. They also would lead Bible studies for children and adults.

Gabe had never been too keen about the ministry aspect of the mission trip, but he was determined to get Stevens off his back. If he didn't go this year, he'd never hear the end of it.

Plus, he had realized in recent weeks what a great marketing tool the trip had become. Along with a feature article in Houston's daily newspaper, a local TV station had asked the mission team to take along a camcorder and record spots that could be shared with their viewers when they returned.

Gabe could take or leave the prayers and Scripture readings, but he knew that was exactly what Stevens was calling about tonight.

"Nothing much is going on here," he told Stevens. "Rachelle is still visiting relatives in Jubilant so I'm just hanging out. Whatcha need?"

"I know you said Rachelle had you all packed; did she remember to tuck a Bible in there somewhere?"

Gabe hadn't seen one, so he was pretty sure she hadn't. "Was that on the list you gave me? Sorry, man. I doubt it."

"You know I've got you covered," Stevens said.

Gabe rolled his eyes. "Look man, I'm not trying to go over there and become a lay priest. I do what I do, and I do it well. Heart stuff.

Internal medicine. That's where I'm going to help. Bible talk—I'm leaving that to you and Chrissa and the other folks."

Stevens chuckled. "You just be ready in the morning, four a.m. sharp. We'll swoop by to pick you up. When you talk to Rachelle, tell her I said hello and reassure her that I'll bring you back safely."

Gabe had hung up and dialed Rachelle's cell again.

She didn't answer, and after the fifth ring, the voice mail picked up. Hearing her recorded voice was reassuring, but he didn't leave a message.

Was he losing her? The thought rattled him. He was Gabe Covington. Couldn't happen . . . could it?

The home phone rang once again, and he dashed to it, only to be disappointed a second time by Lyle Stevens.

"Yeah, man? Why you ringing my phone off the hook?"

Stevens laughed. "What you gonna do about it? I forgot to ask you to let me pray with you, this last night at home before our trip, especially since Rachelle isn't there."

If she had been home, she still wouldn't have thought to pray with him. Stevens knew that, but he was ever the gentleman. Gabe sighed.

Stevens grew serious. "I know you aren't into this Christianity thing, Gabe, but it's a huge part of why we do what we do in the mission field. Let me pray with you, and for you, tonight. It can seriously impact how well our mission trip goes and whether we're able to help a significant number of people."

Gabe sucked his teeth and reclined on the chaise. He kept his eyes open and stared at the ceiling. "Go ahead."

Stevens asked God to protect them during their travels, to allow the medical supplies they had shipped a few weeks earlier to arrive on time, and for the hearts, minds, and souls of everyone they encountered to be open to the transforming power of Jesus. Then, he specifically prayed for his friend.

"Father, bless brother Gabe for agreeing to go on this trip to a foreign land to meet others' medical needs. Thank you in advance for guiding him when he renders a diagnosis and performs surgeries. Give him wisdom as he leads and loves his family with the same love that you show him."

Gabe winced. *Is that the problem? I'm a great doctor but I don't know how to love my family?*

The notion left him uneasy. But when he surveyed the expensive furnishings and accent pieces in his bedroom, and recalled all that he provided for his family, he didn't believe it could be true. Everything that caught his eye disproved that flash of doubt.

When Stevens said "Amen," Gabe quickly said goodbye. He jumped up and headed to the bathroom.

Nothing else to do—so I might as well turn in early, he decided.

After a shower and a slice of cold pizza, Gabe turned on the TV and straddled the bed. He surfed until he landed on a sports channel and settled back on his pillow. Usually he enjoyed having the room and the remote to himself. Tonight, however, he felt awkward lying in this expansive space alone, with nothing but the shadows created by the moonlight to keep him company.

He was dozing off when his cell phone rang.

It was nurse Veronica.

"Hi, Gabe, babe. All packed for tomorrow?" she asked in a sultry drawl. "Ready for our trip?"

What did she want? "I'm ready. Stevens has made sure of that."

"So you got prayed over too," she said and laughed. "He and

his wife are so cute. Surviving this God stuff is going to be the most interesting part of the trip."

Gabe agreed. That and making sure he had a family to come back to. He sat up in bed and pointed the remote at the flat screen TV to turn it off. He reached for the cordless phone on the nightstand.

"Veronica, I'll see you in the morning. I need to call Rachelle."

18

*R*achelle couldn't go home.

She picked up Gabe's message around ten p.m., asking if she could somehow make it home in time to see him off to Uganda.

"If I've pushed you away, I'll do better," he said. "Call me, Rachelle."

If anything, the voice mail message made her angry. When she had settled Yasmin into bed and checked on Indigo, she went into the kitchen and called him back. He answered promptly, but she didn't allow him to speak.

"Gabe, I got your message, but I can't come home. Aunt Irene dislocated her hip in a car accident today and I need to be here for the family. She's having surgery tomorrow."

She didn't tell him that Aunt Irene had been charged with drunk driving or that the accident had left a young boy with a broken leg and arm.

Gabe tried to interject, but she didn't let him.

"Have a safe trip to Uganda. Don't forget to call Tate and Taryn and leave them a message at Mom's and Dad's, if you haven't already talked to them. And about your desire to work things out . . . we'll see, Gabe."

Rachelle sighed and felt the wave rushing toward her again. Where was all of this resentment coming from?

"I can't believe you aren't going to be here for me," Gabe said.

Rachelle frowned. "You sound like a little boy, pouting over a missing toy. I'm not there to occupy you, the kids aren't home, and even Helen isn't around. You don't have anybody to cater to you at the moment, so you're feeling neglected. Well, too bad. Call me when you get back from Uganda and let's see how sincere you are then.

"In the meantime? Can you please ask Lyle and Chrissa to pray for Aunt Irene and for Jillian?" Rachelle asked. "I know they won't just give lip service; they'll actually follow through. Have a good night, Gabe. Be safe."

"Good night, Rachelle. I'll see you when I get back. Take care of yourself and . . . ," Gabe sounded contrite, "come home?"

She hung up without responding. This attitude would earn her an ugly nickname in some circles, but right now she could care less.

Gabe was finally paying her some attention, and for the first time she could recall, she didn't want to be bothered.

Rachelle rose from the table and filled the kettle on the stovetop with fresh water. Some people couldn't live without their coffee; tea was her thing. She always had at least two cups in the morning and two before going to bed.

It had been an emotional day, and she wasn't the least bit sleepy. Hopefully she could make some progress on her Top Ten List, or at least move past number one.

Why is this bothering me so much?

She asked herself that question for the hundredth time as she poured honey into her tea and stirred it with a teaspoon. Was it because Jillian had made the request and she wanted to honor it?

She thought so at first, but in just the past few days, she realized that answer might be too simple.

Jillian had merely opened her eyes to all that she was missing, despite the trappings of wealth and privilege. If she could focus enough to decide what mattered most, maybe she would be able to stop floating through life at everyone else's whim.

The baby steps she had taken so far felt good, but what use was it to push the envelope if she had no road map? Every day she was better appreciating the fragility of life; she didn't feel invincible anymore.

If she didn't do something about it soon, the things she might someday desire would have passed her by.

19

The phone rang nonstop the next morning, with everyone from Aunt Irene's fellow retired schoolteacher friends to Uncle Charles's boss calling to check on her.

Rachelle had forgotten how quickly news spread in a close-knit community. She fielded as many calls as she could before deciding to change the voice mail message.

"Thank you for calling the Burns family. We appreciate your thoughts and prayers for Irene. She is undergoing surgery soon and is expected to fully recuperate. We will update this message as soon as there is more news. In the meantime, please keep the family in your prayers. Thanks and God bless."

Rachelle felt a bit hypocritical recording such a faith-filled message when she barely knew how to pray. She took the ease at which the words rolled off her tongue as proof that she wasn't the only one who could turn holy when the situation called for it. Yet if the need arose, could she have effectively prayed with or for Aunt Irene? She wasn't so sure.

Once the calls began rolling into voice mail, she woke up Indigo and Yasmin and urged them to get dressed. The mother of Yasmin's best friend, Carmen, had called last night and offered for Yasmin to spend the next few days with her family, so Uncle

Charles could concentrate on caring for Aunt Irene. He had accepted the offer and Rachelle planned to drop her off on the way to the hospital this morning.

Indigo was adamant about not needing a babysitter and had sulked for most of the evening, after Uncle Charles told her she couldn't stay home alone all day. From what Rachelle could gather, he normally gave her that option. But he clearly was shaken by Aunt Irene's accident and insisted that this time she go over to a friend's house.

"I'm just not sure how long we're going to be at the hospital, baby," he told her.

She had stomped to her room and avoided him the rest of the night.

This morning, she sat up in bed and told Rachelle she had settled on someone: Troy's niece, Chaundra.

"I really like her, and this would be the perfect way to get to know her better," Indigo said. "Can I hang out with her?"

Rachelle had summoned every ounce of maturity she possessed to keep a straight face. Did Indigo really expect her to call and set this up?

She kept forgetting the girl had no clue. Indigo was born the year that Rachelle and Troy married and divorced.

Rachelle shrugged. She needed to do whatever she could to help right now. This wouldn't kill her. "Did she give you her number? Call her and see what her uncle says."

Indigo's eyes grew wide. "Her uncle? You mean Mr. Hardy isn't her father? Is he single?"

Rachelle put her hand on her hips. "He may be single, Indigo, but he's more than twenty years older than you. Get over it."

The girl giggled and searched for Chaundra's number in her

list of cell phone contacts. She passed the phone to Rachelle. "Can you ask for me? I'm nervous around him."

Rachelle raised an eyebrow. "Maybe you need to find another friend to visit today. You don't need to be hanging around a man you have a crush on, especially since there's not an adult female in the house. I'm not feeling this."

Indigo rolled her eyes. "So now you're saying he's shady? I can't believe this!"

Rachelle took a deep breath and tried to remember how over the top she had been as a teenager. If she couldn't muster some patience, she just might snatch this girl up. "Look, let's remember what this is all about, Indigo—not you. Your mom had a serious accident, she's having surgery today, and we all need to pull together. Call Sabrina or one of your other girlfriends and ask the parents if Chaundra can come over there and hang out with you. I don't have the energy for the drama today."

Indigo sat Indian style on her bed and lowered her head. She muttered something Rachelle couldn't hear and held her hand out for her cell phone.

"Aren't you concerned about your mother? You seemed to be yesterday," Rachelle said.

The wistfulness in Indigo's eyes conveyed more than would ever cross her lips. Just as quickly as Rachelle noticed it, however, it was replaced by adolescent indifference.

Indigo dialed a number and asked to speak to Sabrina's mother. "May I come over for the day and bring a friend who's new to town, Mrs. Robinson?"

When she received the okay, she called Chaundra and looked expectantly at Rachelle, who sat on the edge of the bed, waiting to see how things would unfold.

"Mr. Hardy, good morning," Indigo stammered. "Will you speak to my cousin?"

She thrust the phone at Rachelle, who grabbed it before it hit the floor. She glared at Indigo.

"Uh, hi, Troy, how are you?" She knew he must be thinking she set this up. "I'm sorry to bother you so early, but we're calling to see if Chaundra can hang out with Indigo today, at a friend's house? I'm heading to the hospital with Uncle Charles and we may be there most of the day, depending on how Aunt Irene's surgery goes. Indigo is going over to another friend's house, and that friend's mother has invited Chaundra over too."

Rachelle wanted to kick herself for going on and on, like an eager-beaver teenager.

Troy chuckled. "These young ladies are something else, aren't they? Sure, she can hang out with Indigo today. She'll be excited to meet some other girls too. Should I bring her over to Irene's or drop her off somewhere?"

Rachelle hadn't thought through the logistics. "Let's see, I'm dropping Yasmin and Indigo at their friends' houses on my way to Jubilant Memorial. Do you want me to pick up Chaundra?"

"No, no," Troy said quickly. "You've got enough on your plate. I'll bring her by there, and if you want, I can drop the girls off wherever they need to go. That way, I can introduce myself and Chaundra to the girls' parents."

Rachelle was impressed. For an uncle doing a dad's job, he was on point. But then again, hadn't he always been?

Don't go there this morning.

Her brief self-talk jerked her back on course. "That's a great idea, Troy. Can you be here in about an hour?"

By the time she showered and dressed, Uncle Charles had already left for the hospital. Since Yasmin was raring to go, he had taken her to Carmen's house when he left.

Rachelle grabbed a few magazines and a bottle of water and made sure she had her cell phone, so she could check in with Taryn and Tate before she reached the hospital. Those "No cell phones allowed" signs were plastered everywhere.

She checked her hair and makeup in the mirror, out of habit. Gabe liked her to look flawless, even if she were running to the neighborhood gas station for a refill. He wasn't here to offer a critique, so she gave herself an "A."

She had been in Jubilant just a few days, and already she felt sluggish after missing her Pilates class. Maybe she could walk the neighborhood this evening, if all went well with Aunt Irene's surgery.

"Come on, Indigo! Mr. Hardy will be here in a few minutes."

It felt strange referring to Troy in such formal terms, but Rachelle wasn't sure what he had told Chaundra about her. She intended to downplay their connection as long as he did. At the same time, she was nervous about seeing him again, even if only briefly.

She plopped on the living room sofa to wait for Indigo and glanced at her watch. It was just 8:45, but it seemed so much later, perhaps because she had risen around six a.m.

Thinking about Aunt Irene's accident and the fact that she had been drinking saddened Rachelle. After they helped her work her way through the hip injury, the family needed to address her drinking.

The doorbell rang and Rachelle trotted to answer it. Troy and Chaundra stood there expectantly.

Rachelle opened the door wide and welcomed them in. She hugged Chaundra and led them into the kitchen.

"Indigo left a bag on the table in here with her iPod and a few other necessities," she told Chaundra and Troy. "I want to make sure she doesn't forget it. Are you guys thirsty?"

Instead of joining them at the table, she bustled about, all of a sudden finding things that should be put away or reorganized.

Indigo emerged from her bedroom and greeted her friend. "Thanks for coming over," she told Chaundra. "You remember Sabrina from my party, right? She has a great hangout room at her place."

Rachelle explained that Troy would be dropping them off.

"That's the plan," he said and looked at Rachelle. "Then I'll swing by the hospital and check on Irene."

Rachelle waved him off. "You don't have to do that," she said. "It's nice of you, but I know you're busy. When do you start working on campus?"

"Not 'til the fall semester begins," he said. "But I've been dropping by occasionally, just to get a sense of how the department works and to organize my office."

Rachelle nodded.

"Let's get in the truck," Chaundra told Indigo. "There's a song I want you to hear on my iPod, and I didn't bring it in."

When they were gone, Rachelle and Troy stood facing each other across the kitchen island. Neither knew what to say, but neither looked away.

Rachelle wanted to ask him why he had custody of the girl. No—she really wanted to know whether he hated her for leaving him all those years ago, with nothing more than a note and her half of the rent.

Troy broke the silence. "I couldn't hate you if I tried, you know."

A thrill raced through Rachelle. How had he known what she

was thinking? Then she remembered—he had always known her that well.

The fact that he could still read her expressions after fifteen years, when Gabe had no clue, stunned her.

Troy peered into her eyes and she realized the connection was mutual: she knew what he was thinking and feeling too. He might not hate her, but he needed the explanation she had never had the courage to give him.

She couldn't. If he knew why she left, he just might realize she hadn't been worthy of him in the first place.

She zeroed in on his lips, wondering what it would be like to kiss him again.

"You know, Rachelle, I've forgiven you," Troy said.

Those words chilled her like a splash of cold water.

"I kept holding out hope that you would realize we had something special," he said. "I just knew you would finally wake up and decide that your mom and dad couldn't keep making all of your decisions for you and that you would come back.

"After a while, all I wanted was the reason you just threw us away. But even without that, I moved on."

Tears filled Rachelle's eyes. "I'm sorry, Troy."

She wanted to ask why, if he had loved her so much, he hadn't come after her.

With that selfish thought, she couldn't look at him any longer. She turned her back and wiped away the single tear snaking its way down her cheek. "I was young and stupid and intent on keeping my parents happy, but I didn't realize how much it would cost me."

That was all she could offer him right now. Besides, the girls were sitting in the truck waiting.

As if on cue, Rachelle's cell phone rang and she trotted to the living room to retrieve it from her purse. It was Aunt Melba.

Troy paused in the entrance connecting the two rooms and waved at her as she flipped the phone open. He formed his lips to speak, but instead smiled and left through the front door.

Rachelle watched him go and calculated his assets. He was smart, kind, and talented. He could have been a football star with that physique or a model with that face, but he had never used those qualities to his advantage or been arrogant about what he considered his gifts from God.

"Hello? Helloooo?"

Melba's voice floated through the cell phone and snapped Rachelle back to reality. She was swooning over her first husband and needed both a fan and a wake-up call.

That must explain Melba's timing.

"Are you at the hospital?" Rachelle asked.

"I'm on my way," Melba said.

Rachelle could tell she was using her Bluetooth; she heard air swirling in the background while Melba drove.

"Are the girls squared away for the day or do you need to stay there with them?"

"No," Rachelle said. "I'm on my way too. Both of them will be hanging out with their friends' families for the day, including Miss Grown-Up Indigo, who wanted to stay here by herself."

"Humph," Melba said. "She better get used to not always getting her way. How is she, otherwise? And has anyone talked to Reuben?"

Rachelle hadn't shared Indigo's reaction at the accident scene, but it was just like Aunt Melba to understand that the crash would leave the girl, and Reuben, shaken.

"They both seem fine," Rachelle said. "I talked with Reuben

last night, and he was upset, as expected. I didn't give him any details. All he knows is that Aunt Irene broke her hip and is having surgery."

"Well, we need to get him back on the phone," Melba said. "He needs to know the full story."

Rachelle frowned. "Why? How is that going to solve anything?"

"It may not solve anything, little niece, but it's no secret that Irene was driving drunk. The *Jubilant Herald* has pictures of the accident scene and traffic backup it caused, along with a brief story. It's on the front of the city section and details who was at fault. My dear sister had a blood alcohol level twice the legal limit, and when she crashed into those two cars, she injured a five-year-old boy."

Rachelle's mouth fell open. Uncle Charles had informed them that Aunt Irene had been intoxicated and that a child had suffered minor injuries, but this was bad. Someone did need to break the news to Reuben, and to the girls.

The phone had ceased ringing nonstop about an hour ago. Now Rachelle knew why.

20

*D*espite their awkward encounter earlier, Troy kept his word.

He showed up about two hours into Aunt Irene's four-hour hip replacement surgery and joined Uncle Charles, Aunt Melba, Rachelle, and Pastor Taylor in the waiting room. The folks who had called earlier and told Rachelle they would be stopping by the hospital never materialized.

When lunchtime rolled around, Troy accompanied Rachelle and Melba to the hospital's cafeteria.

"Just the smell of that food makes my stomach turn," Rachelle said as they rode the elevator to the basement.

"You get used to it, and after a while it doesn't faze you," Troy said. He let the ladies step out first, then walked between them to their destination.

Melba raised an eyebrow. "Don't tell me you worked in a hospital too—a singing, mechanical engineer physician?"

Troy threw his head back and laughed. It was contagious. Rachelle and Melba joined in.

"You guys think I'm the bomb, don't you?" he said and grinned.

When they had paid for their sandwiches and claimed an empty table, he explained his earlier comment.

"My mother was diagnosed with colon cancer about eight years ago, so I spent a lot of time with her at the hospital," he said. "So much that a lot of the staff got to know me. I kept telling them I'd sing for a good meal, and one day, they took me up on the offer."

Melba laughed heartily. "I'm so sorry to hear about your mother, Troy. But did I just hear you say you sang for hospital cafeteria food?"

He smiled sheepishly. "I was young and trying to impress people, okay?"

Rachelle read between the lines. Trying to impress the women, he meant to say.

"You weren't that young eight years ago," Rachelle teased. "You're five months older than me, so that would have put you in your late twenties. Come on, now."

He shook his head. "You ladies win, okay? Let's just eat."

They munched on their food in silence for a while, but Rachelle wanted to know more about his mother. "Is your mother okay?" she asked.

"She's in heaven now, but yes, she's okay," he said.

Rachelle's heart went out to him. She wanted to reach for his hand, to comfort him, but knew better, especially on Aunt Melba's watch.

"When she was diagnosed, we moved her to Milwaukee to live with my brother and his family. He had just been hired as an assistant principal there and couldn't come back to Dallas," Troy said. "I was working for an engineering firm that had an office in Milwaukee. I asked for a transfer so I could be there to help."

He looked at Rachelle. "I don't know if you remember my sister."

Rachelle nodded. "Of course. She was very pretty and very bright."

"Tania was a mixed-up teenager when all of this was going on," he told them. "Before the move and Mom's illness, she really got off track, had a baby, and dropped out of high school before graduating."

"Tania?" Rachelle was incredulous.

Troy nodded. "When we moved to Milwaukee, she started dating some thug and wound up on drugs. She's in prison now, serving a seven-year sentence for possession of cocaine."

Rachelle gasped. "Not Tania. Troy, I'm so sorry. How did that happen? She was always so smart and focused when we were dating. I just knew she was going to do great things."

He fixed his eyes on his half-eaten sandwich. "I think she struggled without our father and searched for love in the wrong places. Then Mom got sick, and it was just too much for her. She couldn't handle it, I guess."

"So Chaundra is her daughter?" Rachelle asked.

Troy nodded. "Yeah. We have no idea where her father is. After my sister got strung out, he moved on to his next victim.

"Mom had passed away; my brother's wife was diagnosed with multiple sclerosis and they had three young children; so really, I was the only logical person to take her and prevent her from getting lost in the foster-care system. She's thirteen now and I've had her since she was eight."

Rachelle's eyes widened. "You've been a parent for that long? By yourself?"

She saw the pride in his eyes, and she understood it. He had often talked about the hole punched in his heart when his father abandoned the family.

"With God's grace and wisdom and lots of help from caring friends, I've been able to do it. That's the only way."

Rachelle reached for his hands. "That's really great of you, Troy."

He grabbed her hands and held them. Aunt Melba coughed and warned Rachelle with her eyes.

Rachelle wriggled free from Troy's grip and took another bite of her sandwich.

On one hand, she felt as if she were being stalked by a middle school hall monitor. On the other, she knew that was probably what she needed, especially when it came to Troy.

21

*I*n southern Uganda, the villagers were thankful. For everything.

They uttered *"Webele nyo!"* (Thank you very much!) and *"Webese Kotanda!"* (Thank God!) so frequently that Gabe had become fluent with the phrases.

He was amazed at how thrilled they were to have Americans come to their homes. They treated him and the rest of the team like royalty or long-lost relatives.

He feasted on more mush than he had believed was humanly possible, but he had no intention of complaining or refusing a meal. Each bowl of food was made with care and offered with gratitude by the recipients of his medical expertise. He understood now why Stevens came every year and why this place and these people had stolen his friend's heart.

At night, a peaceful quiet descended on the orphanage where Gabe, Lyle and Chrissa Stevens, and Veronica were staying with others on the medical mission team.

The team members would find a quiet spot to sit by themselves and recount the day's events or exchange advice and encouragement. Chrissa would lead the group in songs that she often performed across Houston with a Christian band.

This evening was no different. Each of the team members shared details about a particular challenge or success they had experienced hours earlier, including how some of them wound up praying for the people they were also trying to physically help. How could you not pray for a child who was wasting away because the lack of antibiotics had caused an infection to spread throughout the six-year-old's body? Or for the grandmother who was dehydrated and refused to eat so that her daughter and grandchildren would have enough food to keep them healthy and strong enough to work?

At some point, the conversation shifted to the team members themselves and how they were faring in an environment so different from home. That conversation led to one about the importance of committed relationships, and how what they were doing in Uganda was modeling for the people they helped how unconditional love and friendships could blossom despite differences in color, culture, and status.

A few team members kept steering the discussion to romantic connections.

"I'm no good at them," Veronica said, and glanced at Gabe. "At least not long-term ones."

"Why not?" Chrissa asked. "That's usually an answer a man would give."

Gabe leveled his gaze at Stevens's wife. "Be careful, woman . . ."

Chrissa laughed. "It's true," she said. "Most guys don't bother to stick through the hard stuff. They want everything to revolve around them, to go their way, to make their world easier." She looked at her husband. "Dr. Lyle Stevens had that same problem, until he met a man named Jesus. Thank ya!"

She threw her hands in the air and threw her head back, causing her blond ponytail to flail behind her.

Gabe bellowed with laughter. Chrissa was a sweetheart, but she needed to give up trying to be hip.

When he had composed himself, he turned to Stevens. "What really changed you, man?"

Stevens shrugged. "Like she said, I met a man named Jesus. When I developed a deeper relationship with him, I realized that when I served and loved my wife, I was serving and loving him."

Something tugged at Gabe's heart. He had never heard a commitment to God described that way.

"You alright?" Stevens asked.

Gabe nodded. "Yeah," he said. "That was just deep."

Veronica's lilting laughter filled the air. She winked at Gabe and smoothed her loose-fitting linen shirt over her ample chest. She had left her cosmetics at home, but even just a hint of lipstick and mascara gave her an exotic look. Gabe knew she wanted him.

The way his wife had been acting, he deserved to be pampered. He craved some attention, but lately, he had desired it from Rachelle.

Gabe stood and excused himself from the group. He ambled toward the edge of the orphanage's enclosed terrace. The area was only partially lit, and he felt less exposed. "Stevens, come here for a minute?"

Gabe stuck his hands in the pocket of his khaki slacks and waited. When Stevens joined him, out of the group's earshot, Gabe asked a question that had been nagging him for several days, since he had witnessed a Ugandan mother bury her sickly infant and another woman squeeze the last of her milk out of a dry breast. The supply of food and water that Gabe and another team member arrived with had left the second mother delirious with joy.

"About this loving and serving stuff, how does that work in the real world?" Gabe asked. He felt awkward asking such a touchy-feely question, but this was his friend.

Stevens draped an arm across Gabe's shoulder. "You finally ready to have 'The Talk'?" Stevens joked. "It's all tied to God, man."

Gabe's stomached clinched. This sounded serious. And holier-than-thou.

He knew he wasn't ready for *that*. But being informed couldn't hurt. Not any more than he already was at the moment.

22

Since Aunt Irene's drunk-driving accident had been detailed in the newspaper, it seemed as if everyone in Jubilant who knew the family was abuzz with disbelief or contempt.

Four days after the incident, she came home from the hospital. Though the house was a single-story rancher, she would be confined to a hospital bed that had been ordered by her doctor and set up in the living room. A physical therapist would visit three times a week to help her regain her mobility.

The only bright spot Rachelle could find in this situation was that school was out for the summer. Yasmin and Indigo wouldn't be forced to face their friends right away. The girls had been hiding out in their rooms and avoiding phone calls since they had returned home after their outings on the day of Aunt Irene's surgery. Chaundra seemed to be Indigo's only friend who hadn't changed with the wind.

Rachelle considered asking her mom to invite the girls to Philadelphia, to share the last three weeks of vacation with Taryn and Tate.

Then she questioned whether helping them escape would be teaching them to do what she had done most of her life—run away from problems. If she stayed in Jubilant for a while, and the family surrounded the girls with support, hopefully they would come through this experience wiser and stronger and better able to cope with life's challenges.

Rachelle had been rising early each morning to prepare breakfast for the family and make sure Aunt Irene took her medicine on time. The first time Aunt Irene heard Rachelle bustling in the kitchen, she protested.

"I want to help," Rachelle insisted. She had to keep telling her, until finally Aunt Irene relented, and even made a request.

"If you need something to do then, would you mind sitting with me in the mornings and reading from the Psalms?" Aunt Irene asked. "This medicine leaves me too weak to hold onto my big old Bible."

Rachelle would read aloud as soon as Aunt Irene woke up and had a cup of coffee.

Because of all that she was facing, from legal woes to disgrace in her church and the community, she told Rachelle the Psalms, penned by David as he endured his own trials, comforted her.

"Can I hear Psalm 91 again?" she asked this morning.

Rachelle complied and unwittingly felt moved by the passage herself, especially the last few verses.

> "Because he loves me," says the LORD, "I will rescue
>   him;
> I will protect him, for he acknowledges my name.
> He will call upon me, and I will answer him;
> I will be with him in trouble,
> I will deliver him and honor him.
> With long life will I satisfy him
>   and show him my salvation."

Aunt Irene nodded and wept as she listened. "God will give me another chance," she said softly.

Rachelle wanted to agree, yet she had doubts.

Why was Aunt Irene equating herself to a person concerned about enemies when she had gotten herself in this mess? She had chosen to drive drunk.

Rachelle wanted to ask someone steeped in their faith about that, someone who wouldn't be put off by her questions. Troy fit that bill, but she had been reluctant to contact him, given Aunt Melba's eagle eyes and stern warning.

Reaching for Troy's hands in the hospital cafeteria had been innocent on her part, but Aunt Melba told her to reconsider.

"What if Gabe had walked in on that? Would he think it was innocent?" Aunt Melba asked. "Or vice versa? If you walked in and saw him holding hands with an old girlfriend, what would you think?"

That question hit home.

She thought about Gabe's nurse, who had accompanied him and the rest of the team on the Ugandan mission trip. Rachelle had admired Veronica at first for agreeing to go and give up her creature comforts for ten days to help others in need.

But like Gabe, Veronica understood what a boost for her résumé this mission experience would be. Rachelle had overheard her sharing that view with a group of nurses at a recent retirement party for a hospital administrator. In the process of raising her profile, Veronica had said, she might actually help a few people.

Rachelle also hadn't been oblivious to the frequent calls between Veronica and Gabe as the trip loomed. She hadn't bothered bringing them up, knowing he would try to explain them away or dismiss her as paranoid. But Rachelle knew a turkey when she saw one. Veronica was ready to gobble up something that didn't belong to her.

Rachelle wasn't sure yet what she wanted from her marriage long-term, but in the meantime, Gabe had better watch himself.

23

*J*ust before sunset, a rainstorm swept through the village and forced Gabe and the rest of the mission team to call it a day.

When they returned to the orphanage, they dispersed for some quiet time before dinner.

Most of the older children who lived in the orphanage were helping prepare tonight's meal, so Gabe took the liberty of lounging on the sofa in their rec room. Sleep tugged at him, but before it won, he mentally tallied up the number of women and children he had examined during the day.

All of the AIDS patients in the area continued to visit the clinics where they routinely received treatment when the missionaries were in town, but Gabe had seen men, women, and children with just about every other kind of ailment.

Some needed the bulk supply of vitamin D supplements he had given them to prevent or slow the progression of rickets. Some needed kits to cure yeast infections. One child had a bug bite that had become grossly infected because it had gone untreated for so long. Gabe delivered two antibiotic shots and, through a translator, instructed the boy's mother how to properly clean the wound.

Their faces floated across his mind's eye, and Gabe felt satisfied, knowing that even on a workday cut short by the weather, he had done some good.

Veronica sauntered into the recreation room and joined him on the sofa. She knew as well as he did that it was inappropriate in Ugandan society for an unmarried man and woman to be alone like this, but Gabe decided not to play enforcer.

"Where's everybody else?" he asked.

She shrugged, curled her feet beneath her, and moved closer. She rested her chin on his shoulder. "What's up, Gabe?"

He frowned and glanced around to make sure no one was coming. "Veronica, what are you doing? We're in a public place! And what are you talking about, 'What's up?' We're done, remember?"

She moved closer. "We don't have to be, Gabe," she said softly and nibbled his ear.

He felt his body betraying him and tried to move away. Veronica grabbed his arm. "I only broke it off because I was tired of being in second place, behind Miss Beauty Queen Rachelle. I didn't mean what I said last month. I just wanted you to think I was going to the medical conference to find another . . . 'friend.' I was being silly and jealous. I'll take you however you want—part-time, full-time, in between. We've been together too long to turn back now, Gabe. Haven't you missed me?"

Before he could respond, she twisted her body and plopped on his lap. She leaned in to kiss his lips and pressed herself into him.

Gabe stood up quickly and she hit the floor with a thud.

"Ow!" She tried to stifle a scream. "What the—"

He scowled at her. "You must have lost your mind. We are on a mission trip, Veronica. With a bunch of Christians, and you are trying this? We agreed that it was over and it is. I . . . I love my wife."

Gabe was surprised by his own admission, but uttering those words helped him realize they were true. He did love Rachelle; he'd just gotten caught up in life, and in acting out the American Dream, as defined by the world at large.

Just these few days away from that environment had begun to open his eyes to something more meaningful. And seeing the partnership Stevens had with his wife, Chrissa, made him wonder what he and Rachelle might be missing.

He glared at Veronica, still sitting on the floor. How had he allowed himself to get entangled with her? With her flawless ebony skin and high cheekbones, coupled with a voluptuous body that she took good care of, she was fine, for sure. A ten from head to toe. But she also was spoiled rotten. If life wasn't going her way, it wasn't going to go anybody's way.

"Yeah, we're on a mission trip, but you and I both said this was more about gaining professional clout than anything else," Veronica reminded him. "Now that you've arrived in this hot and raggedy place, you're really beginning to care? Give me a break, Gabe."

She stood up and dusted off the tight, designer jeans that accentuated her impressive curves. DKNYs seemed so unfitting in a Third World country, but he had realized Veronica was determined to turn heads wherever she could, no matter who she offended. Stevens would be furious when he saw her. He had repeatedly asked Veronica and other women making the trip for the first time to dress modestly, in deference to the culture they'd be entering.

"You don't want this anymore?" she asked Gabe and ran her hand up and down the length of her body, as if she were a *Price Is Right* prize. "I've told you before, someone else will be happy to fill your shoes, baby."

She rolled her eyes and strutted toward the door, where she paused.

"And by the way, if you aren't afraid of what it means to 'dis' me, you need to be. I have your home number and your wife's cell."

24

*R*achelle slid into the driver's seat of her car and started the ignition. Where to?

Uncle Charles had ordered her out of the house for the afternoon to take a break from playing nursemaid, so she had some time on her hands.

She chuckled at her dilemma. How had she gone from scheduling her life around manicures, pedicures, and Pilates classes to serving as Alice from the *Brady Bunch* in a week's time? She was beginning to wonder if she'd feel out of place when she went back to Houston.

After rising every morning to read Scriptures to Aunt Irene, she had decided that she too needed a routine. In her quest to fill her Top Ten List, every night at bedtime she reviewed her day and assessed whether something she had experienced, read, or heard about should become a personal goal.

She could accept returning home a few pounds heavier from lack of exercise and all of this cooking; she had a great personal trainer who would be eager to guide her back into shape. But going back without having done something for herself would equal defeat.

Rachelle pulled out of the driveway and paused at the stop sign.

Left or right? In a town the size of Jubilant, she could take a two-hour leisurely drive and just about cover its circumference.

A car whizzed by with an Everson College "Go Tigers!" bumper sticker plastered on the bumper.

Rachelle smiled. She would visit the campus.

Fifteen minutes later, she turned into the college entrance and slowed the car to a crawl. The changes on campus were amazing. With just ten thousand students, Everson was considered small, but enthusiastic alumni support insured that it continued to thrive.

Some of the streets that she remembered winding through campus had become cul-de-sacs. Plazas and gardens graced the landscape in areas where there had once been nothing but trees or patches of dirt.

Rachelle rounded a familiar corner and smiled when she saw one of her hangouts: the biology building. She had performed more than her share of experiments there and had struggled to cope with a range of interesting lab partners. By senior year, she realized that most of them were introverts who were passionate about their work. If she had been a career counselor, she would have advised them to look for jobs that allowed them to tackle solo projects and succeed.

Rachelle parallel parked next to one of the entrances and quickly unbuckled. She stepped out of her car and approached the door. She wasn't surprised to find it locked. Few science majors took summer classes. Most spent that period gaining valuable experience as interns or on fellowships that could help them create long-lasting networks.

Rachelle returned to her car and pondered her next stop. It didn't take long to settle on McPherson Hall. She had spent so much time in the building that a lot of the other students thought she was a music major.

Rachelle drove the few blocks to that building and parked in the adjoining lot. This section of the campus was surprisingly quiet too. She entered through the familiar arched set of double-paned doors, surprised to find this building as she remembered it. Little had changed since her graduation.

She scanned the long hall, which featured row after row of trophy cases on each side.

Her two-inch open-toe sandals produced a staccato rhythm as she strolled down the path and paused to read brief summaries about the Everson students who had won choir competitions across the South. She knew if she looked closely, she'd find her name and photos. She had helped win at least five awards.

The trophies and plaques spanned generations, as did the pictures—from black-and-white images to color photos that highlighted gospel and choral singers sporting hairstyles and fashions from the '40s, '50s, and '60s through the present.

Rachelle heard voices as she neared the end of the hall and grew excited. Maybe some of her former professors were here today. She waited for whomever it was to round the corner and nearly choked when three people came into view.

Troy and Chaundra approached her, along with a woman dressed in business attire.

"Oh, hello," the woman said and walked toward Rachelle with her hand extended. "Carla Wesson, executive secretary of the music department. May I help you?"

Rachelle found her voice and shook Ms. Wesson's hand. "Hello. Rachelle Covington. I'm a former student, visiting town, and thought I'd stop by."

Chaundra giggled. Rachelle and Ms. Wesson looked her way.

"I saw you on some of those old choir photos with Uncle Troy," she told Rachelle. "Your hair was funny!"

Ms. Wesson looked curiously from Troy to Rachelle. "You two sang in one of the choirs together? You know each other?"

Rachelle nodded. "Isn't it a small world?" she said. "Would it be okay if I continue to look around? I haven't made it to those photos yet. And are any of the professors here today?"

Ms. Wesson shook her head. "No, no one's here today. Wednesday is usually pretty low-key in the summers. But help yourself. Look around. And welcome back, Ms. Covington."

Ms. Wesson turned toward Chaundra. "Did you still need to visit the ladies' room? I'll show you where it is."

"Yes, please," the girl said. She looked at Troy. "I'll be back. Will you be waiting here?"

"Either here or in front of the building, where we came in," Troy said.

When they were gone, he stuck his hands in his pockets and turned toward Rachelle. "How's your Aunt Irene doing?"

Rachelle glanced at him, then focused on one of the trophy cases. "She's at home, but she has a long way to go. Emotionally and physically."

Troy nodded. "That's understandable."

He walked closer and peered at the photo that had captured her attention. Their former choir director, Mr. Pearson, was scowling at the choir and bending toward them, as if he could pull the notes from their throats.

Rachelle and Troy laughed together. Troy leaned against the case and turned to face her.

"I don't believe in coincidences anymore," he said.

"Really?" Rachelle said. "What's that supposed to mean?"

She looked into his eyes and looked away. The longing there scared her.

Troy reached for her hand, but she pulled away.

"Don't," Rachelle said.

She turned and walked down another hallway. Troy caught up with her and reached for her hand again. This time she didn't resist.

Rachelle paused and looked up at him, trying not to get any closer than she already was. What would Ms. Wesson and Chaundra think if they returned right now?

Troy didn't seem to care. He held on to her hand and stared at her.

She thought about the pictures behind them, displaying proud moments and memories made years ago. She wished they could be transported back, to a time when what they both were feeling right now was nothing to be ashamed of or to fear. She wished she could lean into him and hug him, instead of straining in the opposite direction.

Troy kept her hand tucked in his and led her to the end of the hallway and around the corner. "I want to show you something."

She allowed him to guide her.

In the very first case at the edge of the corner were photos from their years at Everson. She recognized the student choir directors in the images. She saw several photos of herself, and one in particular caught her eye. Troy zoned in on it too.

The two of them stood side by side, with their shoulders touching as they smiled and lifted a large trophy in the air. The choir stood behind them cheering.

Troy turned to Rachelle and raised her chin with his forefinger. He held her in that pose for what felt like an eternity. "How did I go from first place with you to last?" he asked. "Why did you leave me, Rachelle?"

He wiped the solitary tear that slid down one of her cheeks

with his thumb and leaned in closer. She should have been telling him to stop, but she didn't.

She let him kiss her, tenderly and slowly, as if he wanted to make it last for a lifetime. She should have pulled away, but she kissed him back.

In a split second, however, she realized she had gone too far. There was no way this could last—no need even faking it. Rachelle pushed past him and trotted down the hallway, toward the main entrance.

"I'm sorry, Troy," she said without turning to look at him, "I can't do this. You can't either. You have too much to lose."

She exited the building and tried to see past the tears that were blinding her.

As much as she resented her husband's lack of attention and affection, Rachelle didn't want to sink lower than he had. She also didn't want to hurt Troy a second time. If he wasn't going to think straight and consider all that he had at stake, she would love him enough to do it for him.

25

*M*osquito netting had become Gabe's best friend. Without the mesh covering to relax and sleep under every night, he was certain from the constant buzzing that filled his ears that he would be returning home with a war story about surviving malaria.

This evening, as most of the other members of the mission team prepared for bed, he and Stevens sat on a screened porch, under a wide swatch of insecticide-treated netting, with the door latched. That had been necessary, because the Ugandans were so fascinated to have Americans staying with and serving them that they rarely gave them time alone, unless it was explicitly requested.

Stevens pulled out an oversized, black leather Bible whose spine seemed nearly gone. He had taped it with masking tape several times; even so, the leather had continued to crack.

"'Bout time to trade that in for a new version, isn't it?" Gabe asked.

Stevens shook his head. "Can't. It holds more than words."

He opened the Bible and slowly flipped through the pages, revealing sections highlighted in yellow or blue, and words or phrases scribbled throughout in ink or pencil. There were dates and partial prayers. Underlined words and question marks.

Gabe snorted. "Is this a textbook or a Bible?"

"Both. I thought the same thing when my grandmother gave it to me just over three years ago, when I got serious about my faith. Most of these markings were made by my grandfather. But when I received it, I bought the highlighter to keep track of passages that spoke to me or that I needed to study more.

"I've found that I'm learning and growing each time I read the same passages," Stevens said. "This book is also a constant reminder of God's goodness and grace."

Gabe folded his arms across his chest.

"What are you thinking?" Stevens asked.

Gabe had questions he didn't know how to pose. How could he be a renowned surgeon and not know these things? Yet, what did he have to lose, thousands of miles from his real world, in a place where time slowed to an ancient pace and joy resulted from one-on-one personal connections rather than being well connected?

"I'm wondering what the difference is between grace and mercy, in the religious sense. You hear Christians spouting those words all the time," Gabe said. "And how can the words in a book change your life?"

Stevens leaned back in his chair. They were so near the equator that the setting of the sun hadn't caused the temperature to dip much. He wiped a trickle of sweat from his brow and stared at the starry sky.

"Grace and mercy are pretty similar," Stevens said. "Grace is God's unearned gift. It means he loves you, he blesses you. He gives you chances you don't deserve.

"When God has mercy on us, he's deciding not to hold a grudge for all of the stupid, mean, or conniving things we've done. It means he gives us a fresh start, with no strings attached, when we ask for forgiveness with a sincere heart."

Stevens glanced at Gabe. Gabe nodded to let him know he could continue. Stevens briefly waved his Bible.

"This book, here," he paused and his voice quivered. "The words in here shook me up, man. When I asked God to take over my life and I read the stories of the early Christians, and about how God's unconditional love was available to me thousands of years later, it changed me."

Gabe looked at his friend. "Is this a white boy thing?"

Stevens frowned, then laughed until he was red in the face. Gabe watched him intently until he composed himself.

"Jesus was born to Jewish parents, had wooly hair, and loved all mankind, Gabe," Stevens said. "I'm laughing because I see that you're serious. You're worried that if you decide to become a Christian here in Africa, you're going to get back to Houston and have to face your friends and family and explain what happened to you. That's it, isn't it?"

Gabe gritted his teeth. Stevens still knew him too well.

"What about all those 'brothers' in Houston, or for that matter, around the world, who profess a love for the Lord?" Stevens said. "Come on, Gabe. You know better."

Stevens was right, Gabe acknowledged. He did know better. But he wasn't about to become some wigged-out Christian, handing out pamphlets and selling all of his goods to move to Africa just because . . . just because . . . He squirmed when he couldn't finish the thought.

Stevens flipped the pages in his Bible until he reached Colossians 3:23–24.

Whatever you do, work at it with all your heart, as working for the Lord, not for men, since you know that you will receive an inheritance from the Lord as a reward. It is the Lord Christ you are serving.

Stevens looked at him. "Serving God doesn't mean you have to change who you are, Gabe," he said. "You just have to allow him to change your heart. When he does that, you can't help but alter the way you treat others, and you'll long to pick up the Bible and know more about him, without having to wait for a Sunday morning sermon. Have I changed that much?"

Gabe thought about it.

Stevens was a different person, but not in an offensive or overbearing way. Instead, he had become more patient and focused on his work, he had become the calming center of the practice when the pace got too frantic, and he seemed much happier.

"You've changed for the better," Gabe acknowledged.

"I'm not required as a Christian to stalk people with my faith, and I hope you've never felt that I've done that with you," Stevens said.

Gabe shook his head. If anything, he had been forced to pull out of Stevens why he seemed content, even when things weren't going smoothly in his personal life or when a patient didn't survive.

"I don't take this big Bible with me everywhere and whip it out for someone in need of a good word," Stevens said. "Some people may do that, but that's not my style. I'll offer to hold their hand, or listen, or pray, when it's appropriate. And sometimes I'll invite them to join me on a mission trip."

Gabe laughed. "I fell for the okey-doke, huh?"

Stevens shook his head and stood up. He laid the Bible on the table in front of him. "I'd never trick you into anything, man. I wanted you to come and help these people that I deeply respect. I wanted you to get a taste of what it's like to live outside your world and your life and your blessings. This experience in and of itself can be life changing.

"This is not a bad place to begin wrestling with God's role

in it all, but honestly, there's no pressure. I've got your back, no matter what."

The men did a soul-brother handshake and hugged.

"How's that for a white boy?"

They laughed.

"Sorry, man," Gabe said.

Stevens was about to part the netting and unlatch the door when Gabe touched his shoulder.

"One more question, man," he said. "About this grace and mercy. Does that apply to everything?"

Stevens turned and faced him. "Before I surrendered to God, I was gambling away my future," he said quietly. "Those long weekend trips I took? They weren't to golf resorts. I was holed up somewhere losing big, while my wife sat at home crying and worrying about whether we'd survive financially. God removed my addiction and saved me from bankruptcy, Gabe. That's nothing but grace and mercy."

Gabe followed his friend into the building and bade him good night.

His mind was swirling from all he'd heard, and he still felt awkward for having asked Stevens to talk with him anyway. He walked to the room he shared with three other men from Gabe's church and tiptoed to his cot, where he would cover himself with more netting and quickly change into lightweight sleepwear.

Once settled, he lay there, listening to the mosquito songs and willing sleep to come. Instead, Stevens's words reverberated in his mind. The portions of the Scripture about pleasing God instead of man became a refrain.

He thought about his sins, the biggest of all being his eighteen-month affair with Veronica. How could he fix that? Would God really help him set things straight?

Stevens hadn't said so, but from the little Gabe knew about God, he realized that if he were going to take a serious step toward faith, he would have to seek forgiveness, not only from the heavenly Creator, but also from his wife.

If choosing God meant Rachelle might never come home, he wasn't sure he could do it.

26

*R*achelle was still flustered by the time she reached Uncle Charles and Aunt Irene's home and didn't want anyone to see her.

She entered through the front door and tiptoed to the powder room, which was conveniently located just before the living room entrance. She closed the door behind her, flipped on the light, and stared at her reflection in the mirror. Her eyes were bloodshot.

I know I did not just lock lips with Troy Hardy.

She wondered whether God was keeping score and if today's offense equaled three strikes all by itself.

Rachelle splashed cold water on her face and patted her eyes, hoping to draw less attention to them. When she felt calmer and able to pretend as if everything were all right, she took a deep breath and emerged from the bathroom.

Voices floating from the living room caught her attention. She crossed the hallway and poked her head inside. Aunt Irene was sitting up on her cot, flanked by Uncle Charles and a well-dressed man wearing a bow tie. Rachelle waved hello.

Uncle Charles motioned for her to join them. "Rachelle, meet John Dupree, our lawyer. He's going to represent your aunt on the misdemeanor stemming from the car accident."

"Oh," Rachelle said. This was the first time they had spoken openly about the charge, although it had been written up in the newspaper. "Is there going to be a trial?"

Mr. Dupree looked in Aunt Irene's direction. "We're hoping for a bench trial, which means the judge will briefly hear the case himself, without us having to select a jury and face a drawn-out process. As soon as Irene feels up to it, I'd like to get her involved in a community service project. That will go a long way toward convincing the judge to be lenient, since this is her first offense. Something not too strenuous, but valuable, to show that she's serious about contributing to society and not making the same mistake."

He waited for Aunt Irene's response.

"I'll go to the AA meetings if you think that will help, John," she told him. "But honestly, I have not had a drop of vodka, or any alcohol, since the accident, and I'm not craving it."

A heavy silence filled the room.

"What?" Aunt Irene asked. She looked from her lawyer to her husband. "You don't believe me?"

Uncle Charles shrugged. "You've made promises before, Irene."

Rachelle was stunned enough to sit on the sofa. Just how long had Aunt Irene been drinking?

"You change for a little while, then you get stressed and run back to your usual crutch," Uncle Charles continued. "What makes this time any different?"

Aunt Irene was fair-skinned enough that Rachelle recognized her embarrassment when she blushed.

"I've never caused a major accident before, Charles," she said softly. "I know how serious this is."

Mr. Dupree rose from his seat and shook hands with Aunt Irene, Uncle Charles, and Rachelle.

"Ladies, gentleman, gotta run to my next appointment," he said. "Call me, Irene, when you've thought about the community service piece, and I'll be researching places as well that might be a good fit."

He left through the front door and closed it behind him. Aunt Irene leaned forward and looked at Uncle Charles.

"So you think I'm still drinking?" she said again to Uncle Charles. "You think I'm that crazy?"

He opened his mouth to say something, but hesitated. He was saved from responding by a light knock at the kitchen door, which was often unlocked when they were home. It creaked open, and though Rachelle and the others couldn't see who had entered, Rachelle knew by the clickety-clack of her stilettos on the kitchen tile that Aunt Melba had arrived.

"Hey, family!" she said.

When she didn't grace the living room right away, Rachelle pictured her poking around in the fridge.

"Rachelle, you didn't cook today?"

Rachelle chuckled. "It's time to go home when Aunt Melba starts showing up, looking for me to prepare a good meal. I don't cook like this in Houston, you know."

Melba entered with a Diet Coke in her hand. "I know—you've got a maid and all. Must be nice. But at least you learned well from your mama. You've got pretty good culinary skills."

Rachelle laughed again. "You're wrong about that one," she said. "I didn't learn how to boil water until I showed up at Everson and Aunt Irene felt sorry for me. She told me I was 'disabled' and made me come over once a month with my friend Jillian to learn how to cook a new dish."

The thought of Jillian made her sad. She hadn't heard anything since her visit to San Diego, but in this case, no news was good.

159

Aunt Melba slid onto the sofa next to Rachelle. The piece of furniture had been shoved against a wall in the living room to better position Aunt Irene's bed.

"What are y'all up to?" she asked.

Uncle Charles quietly left the women to talk.

Irene told her about the lawyer's visit and his suggestion that she find a place to volunteer. Melba took another swig of soda and gave a thumbs-up.

"Got the perfect place for you—Cynthia's pediatric practice," she said.

"What?" Aunt Irene and Rachelle said in unison.

"What would I do with a bunch of cranky, sick little kids?" Aunt Irene asked. "I don't want to go anywhere that's going to leave me blowing my nose or taking my temperature at the end of the day."

Melba waved off her concern. "Cynthia has college students in there all the time, reading to kids in the waiting room, or helping parents understand the various pamphlets she distributes about asthma and other chronic conditions.

"Like I mentioned before, she serves a lot of young mothers, who come to her to get the guidance they're lacking at home. There are a number of things you could do to assist her, Irene. She would welcome you with open arms, and you'd be rendering the kind of community service your lawyer is talking about."

Aunt Irene looked pensive. "But what about my hip? I can get around alright with my crutches or the wheelchair, but I can't be chasing around hardheaded children. I taught high school for thirty years because the younger age groups weren't my cup of tea."

Aunt Melba laughed. "Those babies in Cynthia's office don't want you chasing them. Sitting in a wheelchair, or in one of the chairs in the waiting area, should be okay. Think about it and let me know. I'll call Cynthia if you want to give it a try."

Rachelle touched Aunt Melba's arm. "If she's open to that idea, ask her if I can come too. I haven't done eye exams in a long time, but I'd be happy to help with the routine pediatric eye check-ups or serve as an extra set of hands for whatever else she might need."

The phone rang and Aunt Irene picked up the cordless receiver to look at the caller ID. She raised an eyebrow. "It's Troy Hardy. Wonder what he wants."

Rachelle bit her lip and frowned. Aunt Irene and Aunt Melba both noticed.

"If he's calling for me, tell him I'm not here," Rachelle said.

Aunt Melba cocked her head to the side and stared at Rachelle. "Why would she need to do that? And why would our music director be calling here for his married ex-wife?"

27

Aunt Melba leapt from the sofa and grabbed the phone from Aunt Irene before it stopped ringing. Even in her stilettos, she didn't falter.

"Burns residence," she said. "Hello, Troy. It's Melba. How are you? You're calling for Rachelle? Well, can I take a message for her?"

Aunt Irene frowned and swatted Melba's arm. She motioned for Melba to give the phone to Rachelle, but Melba pretended not to see.

Rachelle wouldn't have been surprised if her heart pounded right through her shirt. What had she started?

"No message?" Melba asked. "You sure? I mean, you took the time to call."

She pursed her lips and nodded. "Got it. I will be sure to tell her. And Troy? Oh, never mind."

Aunt Melba hung up and returned the phone to Irene. She put a hand on her hip and glared at Rachelle. "What is going on?"

"What did he say?" Rachelle asked. "And what was that last exchange about? That whole 'never mind' thing?"

"He said to tell you he was out of line and that he's sorry," Aunt Melba said. "He said to tell you he owes you an explanation. I told him 'never mind' because instead of handling it with him, I'm going to deal with *you*."

Aunt Irene looked at Rachelle. "Where have you been today? What is he talking about?"

Rachelle's face grew warm. She started to squirm. This could not be happening.

"Rachelle?" Aunt Irene said. "Why is Troy calling here for you?"

Aunt Melba moved toward Rachelle and grabbed her by the arm.

"Come on," she said and pulled Rachelle from her chair. "We'll be back later, Irene. Will you be okay?"

Aunt Irene nodded. "Charles is here for the rest of the afternoon. Go on. Get things straightened out. We can't have Troy calling here like this."

Aunt Melba kept her grip on Rachelle's arm and led her outside to her Volvo. She unlocked the car with her keychain device and walked Rachelle to the passenger side, where Rachelle opened the door and plopped in the seat.

When Aunt Melba had settled behind the wheel, Rachelle turned to her. "Why are you treating me like I'm twelve years old? Why are you even getting involved in this? Was that all that Troy said?"

Aunt Melba didn't respond. She put the car in reverse and pulled out of the driveway, steering the two miles to her house in silence. When they reached the beige brick rancher, she ushered Rachelle inside, into her family room. She offered Rachelle a seat on the sofa and returned a few minutes later with a glass of iced tea.

Rachelle sat back and sipped it while Aunt Melba settled on the floor in front of her and began rifling through the lower shelves of a wall-length bookcase.

"What are you looking for?" Rachelle finally asked. "And why did you bring me here to ignore me?"

Aunt Melba finally found what she was searching for—a small black photo album that had been tucked in the back of the bookshelf, behind a row of hardcover novels. She dusted it off and stood up, pressing the album to her chest.

Aunt Melba came over and sat next to Rachelle. She waited until Rachelle set her glass of tea on the table and turned to face her.

"Do you know who you are?"

Rachelle frowned. "What are you talking about, Aunt Melba? And why did you bring me here? To ask silly psychological questions?"

Aunt Melba stared at her for the longest time without responding. Then she passed the photo album to Rachelle.

"You want me to look at your pictures?" Rachelle asked, wondering if Aunt Melba was losing it.

"Rachelle, I've never been married and I've never confronted the regret that must come with being reunited with someone you once loved dearly." Aunt Melba spoke slowly and thoughtfully. "I haven't walked in your shoes, so I have no idea what you're thinking or feeling. But I do know what it feels like to be tempted and to yield to your emotions because it seems right and you think that makes it okay.

"I know what it feels like to wish you could go back to yesterday and fix everything you messed up when you were young and stupid and thought you knew everything. I've been there, and it seems to me that you're heading down that path for a second time.

"Whatever happened between you and Troy years ago needs to stay there," Aunt Melba said. "I'm telling you this because I love you. I know you're struggling in your relationship with Gabe, and coming here and seeing Troy has only clouded the issue further.

But you know what? What you're really struggling with is yourself.

"You have to figure out who Rachelle Mitchell Covington is, behind all of the titles—wife, mother, niece, cousin, friend. What do you want out of life? What is your purpose, independent of the people who fill your life? I'm not saying you don't need those people, but until Rachelle comes to know and love Rachelle, how can she really love anybody else? And until you decide to surrender your heart to God, you might not ever be able to claim a piece of it for yourself. Maybe that's why you're trying to turn back time."

Rachelle lowered her head and closed her eyes. She hadn't yet opened the photo album that she now clutched to her chest.

Everything Aunt Melba said struck a chord. She didn't know who she was. She never had.

That was why it had been so easy for her to give up on a life with Troy when her parents had insisted. She had always been their perfect little princess and hadn't wanted that to change.

That was why she had so readily latched onto Gabe after taking him home one weekend and getting her mother's approval. At least the second time she wed, she got to have a real wedding.

Having the children back to back had been Gabe's idea, as had her membership in Houston's Junior League, Jack and Jill, and other elite organizations that would help them both become movers and shakers in the Houston Metroplex area. Gabe had even chosen her girlfriends, because he happened to associate with or like their husbands.

So who was she really, except a trophy wife with a phat house and a nice bank account—things that, in the long run, could be considered trappings rather than blessings?

Aunt Melba folded her arms and watched Rachelle ruminate.

"Take as much time as you need to think it through," she said. "We've got all night. I just don't want you to leave here and think that running into the arms of an old love is going to make you happy. Troy can't make you happy. Only God can give you that kind of contentment. I know, because he finally showed me that when I was ready."

Rachelle raised herself from her bent-over position and looked at Aunt Melba. Her voice trembled when she spoke. "Troy called because we ran into each other today and he kissed me. No—we kissed each other." Rachelle offered her aunt a sad smile. "Gabe has been indifferent to me forever, and I think he's having an affair. I noticed changes in him and in our relationship a little over a year ago, but I didn't call him on it because I didn't want to throw our lives into upheaval.

"He takes care of home. The kids and I have everything we need . . . except him." Rachelle's voice trailed off as she looked away.

Aunt Melba finished the sentence for her. "So you decided to live with a glass half full rather than risk it becoming empty."

Rachelle raised her eyes to Melba's face. "You didn't know I was so shallow, did you? It can get pretty comfortable living in a place where most of your needs are met. I figured since I had given up the love of my life and my career, I could at least have everything else."

"But how does that make you feel about you? How do you feel about the fact that Gabe isn't faithful to you?"

Rachelle looked away again to avoid Aunt Melba's searing gaze. "I really don't know. I tucked my feelings away, I guess, so I wouldn't have to experience the pain and rejection that had become the norm. I started functioning inside the new reality and didn't examine it too closely."

Aunt Melba held out her hand. "Let me see the photo album." She took it from Rachelle and opened it. "This is one of my favorite pictures."

She pointed to a photo of herself clad in a strapless royal purple gown. She was standing next to a tall, muscular man dressed in a white suit and purple cummerbund. They were hugging and grinning at the camera.

The next photo showed them clad in bathing suits, kissing under a waterfall. In a third picture on the page, Melba and the man sat on a sofa and she was resting her head on his lap, eyes half closed.

"I loved him," Melba said and sighed. "But he couldn't love me back."

Rachelle squinted at the photos then gasped. "Is that . . . ? Isn't he married?"

Melba looked at Rachelle. "Yep, that's the mayor. We were together before he became mayor, during his tenure with the city school board. Very married. With children, the house, the dog, and me, a long-term concubine."

Rachelle cringed. "Why, Aunt Melba? You're beautiful. You own your own business. Nothing was holding you back. You could have had anybody. Why settle for a married man?"

Aunt Melba gave her a pointed look. "Why do any of us settle, Rachelle? I was in between serious boyfriends at the time and flattered by his attention. I didn't realize he was married when we first began dating, and by the time I discovered his status, after our fifth or sixth date, I was smitten. He told me the usual—he was staying there for the kids, he didn't love her, she didn't have his back—and I wanted to be there for him."

She released a dry laugh. "And I was there for him, for five years."

Rachelle gasped. "That long, Aunt Melba? How did you hide it?"

She shrugged. "When you're in love, or accept what masquerades as love, you'll do whatever you have to do. We were never together in public, but we'd travel solo to island locations and other vacation spots and meet there. He would come here to my place after nightfall and leave out of the back door in the early morning hours. We had a system, and it worked."

Rachelle's mind was reeling. She wanted to know what this had to do with her, but she also wanted to know what happened. Aunt Melba was good at reading her face.

"By the fourth year, I was tired of playing the game," she said. "I wanted to settle down. I wanted to start a family. I wanted a life.

"But he already had one," she said and laughed softly. "That's when I realized I was just another trinket, another hobby. I started to wake up and understand that I had been sleepwalking through life. I didn't know who I was or what I wanted. I needed to find me so I could love me."

Rachelle sat back and grabbed a pillow to hug.

Aunt Melba continued. "When I began to change, he stopped coming around as much. I didn't push him away because I was still attached to him. I still loved him, and some part of me was holding out hope that he would eventually realize that we belonged together.

"About that time, two things happened. I found out I was pregnant, and when I told him, he went ballistic. He insisted that I get rid of the baby, and I was stunned. I couldn't believe that he wanted me to kill something that was part of both of us."

Rachelle glanced at Aunt Melba and tried to keep her disbelief from spreading across her face. Melba had always been the one who had it together—style, business savvy, self-confidence. How had she hidden all of this muck beneath the image she portrayed?

Aunt Melba stood up and paced the floor while she went back in time. "Irene noticed a change in me, but I wouldn't tell her what was going on. She and Charles had begun attending St. Peter's, and she kept bugging me to visit . I went the Sunday after Elvin told me that he wanted me to abort our child. I was just broken inside."

She sat next to Rachelle and looked out of a window. "The minister that day preached about the woman at the well, who had been married to five men and was living with another man who wasn't her husband. Jesus offered her a chance to follow him, to fall in love with him so that she'd never feel empty and lonely again.

"I wanted that for myself, Rachelle. I decided that day to start over."

Rachelle leaned forward and looked at Melba. "What happened with Elvin and with the baby?"

Melba looked at her and took a deep breath. "I stopped seeing Elvin, and I lost the baby. Two days after deciding to live for God, I was opening the salon and I started bleeding. I drove myself to the hospital where I had a miscarriage."

She picked up the photo album again and flipped to other pictures of herself and her married friend. "If you look at these images, our smiling faces don't tell you all of these stories. You don't know that he's someone else's husband and that we're sneaking around, creating a pretense of happiness. You don't know that he's breaking his vows and that I'm not as fulfilled as I appear. It's all a façade, Rachelle, and many of us live that way until we decide to wake up."

"Yeah," Rachelle said, "but what does waking up cost you?"

Aunt Melba shook her head. "I think the more important question is, what does it cost you to remain half whole? That's why I brought you here today. I don't know what all is going on between you and Troy, but it's obvious that you two are at a crossroads, and before you take a plunge off a cliff, I had to at least warn you.

"I also don't know what's going to happen with you and Gabe—that's between you, him, and God. But nothing needs to happen with Troy or with anyone else until you look in the mirror and figure out what's going on with Rachelle. Now is the time."

Rachelle hugged her aunt and didn't let go. Melba was right. This was it. Who was she going to be?

28

*R*achelle could tell her heart was softening because God had begun answering her prayers.

As she had requested, Troy's participation in St. Peter's service this morning hadn't forced her to maintain a plastic smile for three hours.

When he stood in front of the Inspirations choir and led them through a powerful rendition of David Lawrence's "Encourage Yourself," she had been able to focus on the message in the music instead of on him. She had fretted about being under the scrutiny of St. Peter's members who had discovered her connection to Troy, but she should have been more concerned about what folks were saying about Aunt Irene.

Alanna had driven down from Dallas yesterday and had accompanied her to church this morning. The sisters purposely sat near the back of the sanctuary, where they saw heads leaning together so people could whisper when Uncle Charles led the deacons in collecting the offering.

A few people rolled their eyes and others pursed their lips when he reached their pew to pass the plate. He shared his usual polite greeting and seemed unfazed, but Alanna was boiling.

"Can you believe these Holy Rollers?!" she whispered. "This is why I rotate churches every six months. Just when you start to get comfortable and believe they're sincere, they go to showing you their ugly sides. I never give 'em the chance to hurt me!"

Rachelle sat back and looked at Alanna. Since when had this diva found time to sit still in somebody's church? Had she really visited one place for as long as six months without telling her big sister?

Alanna caught Rachelle's gaze. "What?"

Rachelle chuckled and shook her head. "We'll talk later."

Yasmin tapped Rachelle on the shoulder and asked to go to the bathroom. Indigo, who had been sulking the entire service, interceded and grabbed Yasmin's arm.

"I'll take her."

She and Yasmin slid out of the pew, past Chaundra, before Rachelle could respond. Her heart went out to the girls, especially Indigo. What fifteen-year-old wanted the notoriety of having a mother who drove while tipsy and caused an accident that injured another child?

Yasmin's play dates had dried up, even with her best friend Carmen, but it had been harder for her to understand why her mommy's accident was causing these problems.

Rachelle noticed when they arrived at church this morning, for the first time since the accident almost two weeks ago, that the same girls who had huddled around Indigo at her party were now treating her like she was contagious. Indigo had been careful not to look their way; she knew what to expect.

Chaundra had spoken to the girls in the group, but walked past them to sit with Indigo and Yasmin. However, even that hadn't lifted Indigo's mood. Both girls sat with their heads lowered for most of the service and focused on writing in or reading their bulletins.

After the offering, Pastor Taylor announced that in two weeks, the eleven a.m. service would double as an installation program, just for Troy.

"We'll have our usual choir selections and other participation by the members," Pastor Taylor said, "but a guest minister will render the message, and after the offering, I and other ministers Troy has invited to participate in this special service will pray over him and formally install him as St. Peter's music director. Amen, church?"

Rachelle, Alanna, and their young cousins remained seated after the service and waited for Uncle Charles to finish counting the offering with the other deacons. Chaundra hugged Indigo and left with a young family who had asked her to babysit.

None of the girls' other friends or their parents approached them to ask how Aunt Irene was doing. When Rachelle made eye contact with the women's ministry leader, whom Aunt Irene raved about all the time, the woman turned her head and made a hasty retreat.

Troy stood at the rear of the church next to Pastor Taylor, shaking hands with members of the congregation as they departed. Rachelle averted her gaze when two women approached Troy together and took turns fawning over him. The petite one was dressed to kill in stiletto sandals and a form-fitting lavender dress. The other was tall and thick. She wore black slacks and a green silk blouse that draped her frame perfectly.

Guess they're going to let him *choose whether he likes "Minnie Mouse" or a sister with big bones,* Rachelle mused.

Rachelle, Alanna, Indigo, and Yasmin were still waiting for Uncle Charles by the time those ladies and all of the other churchgoers had departed.

Pastor Taylor came over and hugged each of them, and Troy

followed his lead. When Troy reached Rachelle, he hesitated but took her lightly into his arms.

She tried not to squirm when he embraced her. It amazed her that, after all these years, he still had that effect on her.

Pastor Taylor sat on a pew across the aisle and called Indigo and Yasmin over to chat with him.

Troy looked into Rachelle's eyes. "You doing okay?"

Alanna, who stood next to her sister, cleared her throat. "Yeah, we are, Troy, thanks for asking."

Rachelle wanted to kick her. An attitude wasn't necessary all the time.

Troy took Alanna's hands. "I'd be angry too, Alanna, if my family had been snubbed like yours was today. People sat through an entire sermon in which Pastor talked about the need to love others beyond what we think we can humanly do. They said "amen," they clapped at all the right times. Some even shouted. But how many came over to you two or to Indigo and Yasmin and offered a hug or asked if they could pray for you or for Ms. Irene?"

Alanna stared at him without responding. Rachelle saw that her sister was taken aback by his straightforwardness.

"I'll tell you what, though, Alanna," he continued. "What I've learned over the years is that it isn't about them anyway. God gave them a chance to replicate his love and mercy today, and from what I saw, not one of them took him up on the challenge.

"But in the end, will either of you do it? Will the girls or Deacon Charles? The next time you encounter someone who has made a serious mistake, will you be willing to love them instead of judge them? I guess that's the whole point of this for you."

Troy released Alanna's hands and gave her a hug. He looked toward Rachelle as if he wanted to say something, but nodded instead and walked toward the rear of the church. Pastor Taylor

174

had left through the same hallway seconds earlier, and Rachelle was guessing Troy didn't want to be left behind.

"Hang tough, ladies, it'll get better," he said.

"How can you be so sure, Mr. Hardy?" Indigo called out after him. Her voice trembled, and her eyes were red.

Troy paused and turned toward her. He glanced at Rachelle before responding. "I've been in a pit similar to the one you're in now, Indigo. Feels like the snakes are biting and no one understands. You're hurt and angry at the same time. Embarrassed. Humiliated, and yet you have to go on. You have to."

He spread his arms wide, eagle-like. "I'm walking proof that no matter how much someone hurts you, God can make things better." He looked at Rachelle again, then disappeared down the hallway.

She wanted to run after him and tell him that she understood his pain, because it mirrored her own. They were always going to love each other. They just had to figure out how to do it from afar.

29

*H*ave you won the lottery or are bill collectors trying to find you?"

Rachelle laughed and closed the book she had been reading aloud to Aunt Irene. "Neither, Auntie. This must be 'Catch Up with Rachelle Day,' though."

She had ordered J. California Cooper's latest short story collection from an online bookstore, and when it arrived three mornings ago, she pulled it out when she finished reading from the Psalms.

Aunt Irene loved the stories. She and Rachelle discussed the characters and chatted about what they would do if they were in those fictional situations.

It was becoming an enjoyable part of the morning routine for both of them, but today, the incessant ringing of Rachelle's cell phone had distracted them. She hadn't picked up every call, but the few people she had chatted with briefly reminded her of her full life back in Houston.

"Every day when I pass by your place and see the wrought iron gates closed, I wonder if you're still living there," said Kit Basque, her neighbor and tennis partner. "Is everything still alright in paradise, dahling? That handsome man hasn't locked you out, has he?"

Her tinkling laughter was meant to convey that the question was a joke, but Rachelle had long been able to see the real Kit. Whatever she decided about her future, this woman would be the last to know.

"Sorry, you can't get rid of me that easily," Rachelle responded with her own lighthearted chuckle. "Get your tennis game together. I'll be home soon."

Shelley, Trina, and Jade called next and put her on speakerphone. They sat in the back of a limo, traveling home from the airport, and were calling from Jade's cell.

"Barbados was fabu, girl!" Shelley said. "You don't know what you missed!"

"We'll send you pictures, though, so you can see," Jade chimed in. "Next time don't tell us no! Instead of having fun with your girls, you're down there in that lifeless little town, where cable TV is probably the biggest form of entertainment. What are you doing anyway? Eating everything in sight and getting fat?"

The three women giggled.

"Actually," Rachelle said, "I am doing a lot of cooking. My aunt was injured in a car accident and I'm taking care of her."

"Girl, isn't that what home health aides are for?" Trina said. "Get her some help so you can come home! I know you probably need another makeover after being down there. You disappeared from Houston before we left for our cruise. We're back and you're still gone!"

Rachelle glanced at Aunt Irene, who was occupying herself with the book's jacket while she waited for the call to end. Her life just a few hours away seemed so distant now. She hadn't mentioned her friend Jillian to the three of them, and listening to them now, she realized they wouldn't understand.

Drinks and a massage would have been their prescription—one

she had happily adhered to for years. Now, she wasn't so sure that would satisfy her. She was beginning to question in which world she fit.

"Ladies, I've got to run," Rachelle said. "I was right in the middle of something with my aunt. I'll be home soon and promise to call so we can get together, okay? I'm glad the trip was wonderful!"

She hung up just in time for her housekeeper Helen's ring.

"Hey, Mrs. Covington," she said. "Just touching base to let you know that nothing important has come in the mail. House is still spic and span from last week, since no one has been home."

Rachelle wondered if she was hinting for another week of paid vacation.

"I'm sure it is still clean," Rachelle said. "Probably very little to do without the family underfoot, huh? Actually, though, it's nice to have you there, Helen, just so the neighbors won't think the place has been abandoned. Thanks for stopping by a few times during the week."

The next time the phone rang, Aunt Irene chuckled and closed the book. She lay back in the bed and closed her eyes while Rachelle took a call from her kids.

"Mommy, tell Gram that you let us have more than two cookies for dessert sometimes."

Rachelle sighed and shook her head. When it got down to nitpicky things like the number of cookies one could have, the summer vacation was wearing thin. Then again, Rachelle knew how controlling her mother could be. About everything.

"Put Gram on the phone," she told Taryn.

"Hey, Mom," Rachelle said. "What's the latest drama?" She'd be able to assess the weight to give the phone call based on her mother's response.

"This little girl does not need any cookies, let alone three," Rita Mitchell said. She lowered her voice, "I know her little pudgy self has gained five pounds since she's been here, and I haven't been letting her eat more than one serving of anything."

Rachelle wanted to blow, but already knew how ineffective that would be. She took a deep breath and measured her words. "Mom, Taryn is eight years old," she said. "Eight! Not eighteen. Please don't restrict my child's diet. She is a growing girl. I'm sure you are providing her with healthy meals, so let her have more, within reasonable limits, okay?"

She wished she could see her mother's face, but knew it was clouded with indignation.

"That's why all of these children have an obesity problem today," Rita Mitchell said. "Parents can't tell them no. I never let you have too many sweets or soda or stuff like that."

"There were a lot of things you didn't let me do," Rachelle said. "Too many, in fact."

Aunt Irene opened her eyes and raised an eyebrow. Rachelle noticed and decided to end the call.

"Mom, you do what you think is best," she said. "Just remember that they're kids. I'll call later tonight to check on them."

Rachelle hung up, turned back to Aunt Irene, and picked up the book. "Mom said to tell you hello and she hopes you're feeling better."

She resumed reading and made it to the end of the section before another call came through. She didn't recognize this number, though, and decided to ignore it.

"Go on and take your calls, Rachelle," Aunt Irene said. "I can't go anywhere; I've got all afternoon to finish the story and chat about it."

Still, since she wasn't familiar with the number, she let the call roll into voice mail.

Seconds later, a light flashed, indicating that she had a message. Her patience was wearing thin as she punched in her voice mail password.

She stopped breathing as she listened.

"Rachelle, bet you didn't expect to hear from me," the voice said. "Just wanted to let you know that I'm here in Africa with your hubby, making sure he gets all of his safari needs met, just like I always do. And I do mean all of them. Hope you're enjoying the weather in Texas."

The woman hadn't left her name, but she didn't have to. Rachelle knew Veronica's voice.

Rachelle clutched the book in her lap and stared out of the window. Her thoughts tripped over each other.

So it was true—Gabe was having an affair and Veronica was his mistress. How long had this been going on? She had suspected something, but she wanted to be wrong. Even after her talk with Aunt Melba, she had dismissed her suspicions as paranoia. But maybe this call wasn't legitimate. Veronica could simply be trying to rattle her. Would Gabe really be bold enough to take his girlfriend on a Christian mission trip?

Aunt Irene had been right all along. Gabe was a selfish, self-centered man, and there wasn't anything she could do to change him. If he really had stepped out on her, and if she had any shred of self-respect, there didn't seem to be any more reason to even try to make it work.

30

*R*achelle strained to compose herself without burdening Aunt Irene with the details of the last call, but Aunt Irene knew something was awry.

"Want to talk about it?" she asked.

What Rachelle really wanted was to crawl into bed, curl into a ball, and stay there forever. She wanted to be alone so she could throw something. And cry.

Instead, she tried to feign interest in the third short story in the collection.

Aunt Irene patted her hand. "You go on and take a walk or something. Something's got you distracted. Get away and talk to God about it."

Rachelle graced her aunt with a halfhearted smile. "Does God hear heathens?"

She was thinking about Troy, their kiss, and how she had enjoyed it. If Veronica was telling the truth about Gabe, though, her transgression hadn't been so bad.

"Does he hear heathens?" Aunt Irene repeated the question and raised her hands heavenward. "I sure hope so, cause you lookin' at one. After I have shamed my family and hurt someone else's child by driving drunk, God has every right to forget my name and address, like it seems most of my friends have."

Her eyes filled with tears. "And Reuben."

Rachelle took her hand. Reuben had called several times from Prairie View, where he attended college and was enrolled in summer school classes. But she was surprised that he hadn't made the two-hour trek home, especially after Aunt Irene underwent surgery. Rachelle had been tempted more than once to ask what was going on, but had thought better of it.

Aunt Irene continued. "If God can love me and heal me in spite of myself, if he can hear my prayers and send me the peace I've begged for, he can hear you too, Rachelle. I could tell that last call unsettled you. Whatever it is, give it to God."

Rachelle sighed. "That sounds so easy—'Give it to God.' What does that accomplish? What does that even really mean?"

Aunt Irene tried to sit up on her elbows. Rachelle stood up and propped a couple of pillows behind her.

"It means you tell God what you desire to happen in a particular situation and you ask him to make the best decision on your behalf," Aunt Irene said. "Then you just stop worrying about it, do the best you can with the options and opportunities available to you, and let God work it all out. He's the only one in control anyway.

"Believe me, that's easier said than done. But after lots of practice, you eventually learn to really let go and trust him. I'm not a pro at this myself. There are things I'm still working through. But I know God is in the fight with me."

Rachelle began to weep. "What if you're too angry to turn it over? What if you just want to hurt the person who hurt you?"

Aunt Irene leaned forward and took her hand. "Whatever it is, Rachelle, you have to feel the pain, then let it go. It will eat you alive if you don't. You have to work through the anger, then forgive and determine what's next. Forgiveness is always key. You have to release yourself and the other person."

Rachelle wiped her eyes and looked at Aunt Irene. "I don't understand. When I sit with you, you share all of this wisdom and helpful advice. Then I find out you're out somewhere drinking too much and driving. Which Irene can I trust?"

It was Aunt Irene's turn to tear up. "I deserve that," she said. "When I look in Indigo's eyes, I can tell she's asking herself the same question: which Mama does she really know, and which one can she rely on?

"I fell into drinking years ago, after David and Meredith died. Losing my only son left a hole in my heart that hasn't healed to this day."

Rachelle sat back in her seat. Now she understood.

"When I got the call that he and Meredith had been killed instantly on the Gulf Freeway, part of me died too." Aunt Irene squeezed her eyes shut to staunch the looming tears. "But I had to keep it together for his kids. Reuben was twelve, Indigo was seven, and Yasmin was just eight months—not even old enough to remember anything about her parents.

"I had to wipe their tears and provide them with whatever they needed to make it through the loss. I stopped being their grandmother in order to raise them, Rachelle, and when I did that, I didn't have a chance to grieve."

Rachelle climbed onto the bed next to Aunt Irene and hugged her.

"I accompanied Charles to his company Christmas party about a year after the accident, and one of his bosses gave me a glass of champagne to toast Charles for being named the top car sales-man of the year," Aunt Irene said. "I sipped it at first, then a waiter walked by and offered me a second one. When I drank part of that, I felt a little buzz. I realized that for the first time in what seemed like forever, my heart wasn't aching. I could think about losing David and never seeing Meredith again and about the tragedy of it all for my grandchildren and feel numb. Numb was better than the pain."

Rachelle did the math and looked at her. Reuben was twenty.

"This started almost eight years ago?"

Aunt Irene nodded. Rachelle could tell the confession was helping her.

"That's what your Uncle Charles was referring to when John, the lawyer, was here." Aunt Irene removed her glasses and rubbed her eyes. "He's seen me cycle on and off alcohol several times since then, usually when I'm stressed. I've always hidden it well—I'm a deacon's wife, you know?

"I usually could pull myself together and quit on my own. The hip injury last year threw me for a loop, though. Nothing the doctors gave me would dull the pain. I tried the vodka one day and it worked, and there I went again."

"What happened on the day of the accident?" Rachelle asked.

Aunt Irene sighed. "I mixed my prescription medicine with the alcohol. I had scrubbed the kitchen floor late the night before, after the barbecue. Because I had been drinking, I didn't realize just how much I was moving my hips.

"That Monday morning, the pain was so fierce I wanted to scream. My hips felt like they were on fire. I took my anti-inflammatory medicine as usual, but this time, I also took a prescription painkiller. Then I had the nerve to chase it down with my usual morning drink—the vodka."

Rachelle nodded. "Yeah, that would leave you impaired. But where on earth were you going?"

Aunt Irene shook her head. "To tell you the truth, I really don't remember. I recall thinking I was hungry. I believe I was headed to the Chinese place on Thompson Avenue. Or maybe I wanted to go to the cleaners. There's no telling."

Aunt Irene looked sunken and sad. She lowered her eyes and surveyed her hands while she let her revelations sink in. Rachelle hugged her again.

"Are you addicted, Auntie?"

Aunt Irene shrugged. "I don't think so, but then again, why would I be drinking early enough in the day to crash a car at one p.m.? I haven't had a drink since the accident and I haven't craved one, but I'm also on prescription pain medicine now, for the hip injury, versus over the counter."

Rachelle sighed. "Professional help is available if you really need it, you know? You'll get through this. You'll be fine."

Aunt Irene nodded. "I think so," she said. "But now you know why Reuben rarely comes home. He thinks I'm a hypocrite and can't stand that Charles tolerates it. And look how Charles and the girls are suffering because of me.

"I'm wondering if he's selling any cars these days, or if people are shunning him at work too. He won't say. Yasmin, she's so young and unaware, she loves me unconditionally. Indigo can't stand to be in the same room with me. I'm really worried about her."

"It's going to all work out, Auntie," Rachelle said. "Isn't that what you're always telling me faith is about? I just want you to get better, and if you need it, get some help so this doesn't happen again."

"It won't, Rachelle. I know how much is at stake," Aunt Irene said. "I don't mean to change the subject, but I hope you do too."

31

The neck that had once enticed him with forbidden longing now drew his attention for a different reason. Gabe was so angry that he wanted to choke the life out of Veronica.

She couldn't be telling the truth.

"Don't believe me? Call your wife and ask her what she knows," Veronica said and laughed. "Call her and ask her who she believes."

A caretaker at the orphanage joined Gabe and Veronica outside and began peppering them with questions about American life. What was Hollywood like? Was everyone really rich? How did poor people survive? Had they ever met Beyoncé or Barack Obama?

Gabe politely excused himself from the conversation and assured the man that Veronica would be happy to tell him everything he wanted to know.

"She's a big fan of *Entertainment Tonight* and the *National Enquirer*," Gabe said with a straight face. "I don't think she has to be anywhere this afternoon. Ask away!"

Veronica narrowed her eyes at Gabe while smiling at the caretaker, who led her to a bench where they could sit and chat.

That's what she deserves, he thought. *First she seduces me, then she tries to ruin my marriage.*

All he could think about was Rachelle hearing Veronica's accusations and being devastated. Despite the disdain he had long felt for his wife, he had never meant to hurt her. Veronica had just been . . . available.

He strolled through the orphanage, looking for a quiet, secure spot in which he could make a cell phone call. Sometimes the calls went through and sometimes they didn't.

He wondered where Veronica had been when she succeeded in contacting Rachelle. How could she?

He finally got through and decided to play it cool, in case Veronica had been bluffing. When Rachelle didn't answer, he left a message on her voice mail.

"Rachelle, I'm guessing you're still in Jubilant, and . . . that's fine. Just wanted to say hi and let you know that things are going well here in Uganda. We have a few more days left before we head back to the States. The trip has been . . . amazing, Rachelle. I can't wait to see you and tell you about it."

God, please don't let her leave me.

He left a similar message at home, in case she had decided to return to Houston. What if she were at their house, moving herself and the kids out? The more he thought about losing his family, the angrier he grew. It was all that selfish Veronica's fault.

Before fully thinking it through, he stalked off in search of her. She was still on the patio, this time sitting by herself. Gabe moved swiftly, until he was standing before her.

"Do you know what you have done? You may have ruined my life! You think that's going to make you Mrs. Covington? Think again!"

Veronica couldn't escape him from her seated position, so she cowered instead. "Stop yelling," she hissed. "All these folks don't need to know we've been sleeping together!"

"Too late."

Gabe spun around and Veronica leapt to her feet.

Stevens stood before them, and he was fuming. "I really don't believe this." He looked at Gabe with a mixture of hurt and disgust. "Man . . . why?"

Gabe lowered his head.

Veronica stepped in front of him and smiled at Stevens. "So now you know." She stabbed her finger in Gabe's direction. "Your partner here has been stringing me along for almost two years, telling me how bored he is with his Barbie-doll wife, and how he needs some true companionship. Well, I'm tired of playing second string. He needs to make good on his promises."

Stevens looked from Veronica to Gabe and back again, without speaking.

He bowed his head briefly before looking up again and gently addressing Veronica. "This trip ends in another four days, but under the circumstances, especially since our hosts have likely heard this inappropriate exchange, I think it would be wise for both of you to head back home early."

Veronica seemed unfazed. "I'm tired of this place anyway," she said. "Please send me home!"

"The thing is, I can't send you out of here together—that would be just as inappropriate as allowing you to stay. One of you has to go tomorrow and the other can leave two days later. It's going to be an extra burden for our drivers to keep going back and forth to the airport two hours away, but I don't see any other way to handle it."

Gabe sighed and shook his head. Not only had he broken his marriage vows, he had disgraced himself with his colleague.

Mukasa, the director of the orphanage slowly approached Stevens and tapped his shoulder. He took Stevens aside and gestured vividly while speaking too low for Gabe or Veronica to understand.

Gabe looked at her and rolled his eyes. "Happy now?" he asked. "Feel better?"

She rolled her eyes as well. "If I can't be happy, neither should you. We went into this together, so we can go down together."

Stevens and Mukasa returned. Mukasa lowered his eyes so that he did not have to look at either Gabe or Veronica. Stevens addressed them matter-of-factly.

"Mukasa can arrange for you to stay in a nearby parsonage with a minister and his wife for the next four days," he told Veronica. "That would prevent us from burdening his drivers with extra trips. It's more feasible for you to go than Gabe, because the family has three daughters. You are the more appropriate choice for their sleeping arrangements."

Veronica put her hands on her hips and glared at him. "You're trying to send me off to sleep in some hut? In Africa? By myself? Who do you think I am?"

Stevens sighed and turned to Mukasa. "Thanks, friend, but we're going to have to figure something else out, okay?"

By nightfall, it had been determined that Veronica would stay, but would no longer serve in the same vicinity as Gabe. As long as they weren't seen together, Mukasa agreed to tolerate their presence for the duration of the trip.

Stevens had been sullen the rest of the day. Gabe finally garnered the courage to approach him after dinner, where he sat with Chrissa, looking out into the bush.

Gabe walked over slowly and stood there, unsure of what to say.

After what seemed like an eternity, Stevens broke the silence. "Yes?"

Chrissa patted his back and rose from her seat. "I'll leave you two to talk."

Before walking away, she paused and gave Gabe a light hug. "No matter how bad it seems right now, all things have a way of working themselves out."

Gabe didn't tell her that was what worried him most. When she was gone, he took her spot next to Stevens.

"You disgusted with me?"

Stevens looked at him. "Yeah, Gabe, I am. How long has this been going on?"

Gabe sat back and peered up at the sky. "Veronica exaggerated a little. I'd say about eighteen months. Either way, it was too long. The other night, when I was asking you about God's grace and mercy? It was because of this. Veronica and I broke up about a month or so ago, and my stay here only reinforced that decision. She kept coming on to me and got angry when I told her it was really over. I lost it earlier today when she bragged about calling Rachelle and telling her about the affair. Is this how God redeems our mistakes?"

Stevens stood up and faced Gabe. "Don't go bringing God into this. You're no scapegoat. We all have to deal with the consequences of our actions, no matter who we are—saved or sinner. You still need to ask him to forgive you, along with asking Rachelle—and Veronica, for that matter—if you're serious about fixing things."

"Veronica?" Gabe said and frowned.

"Yeah, her too," Stevens said. "I don't know how all of this started, but you chose to participate. You chose to cheat on your wife, and in the process, you violated Veronica too. If you had resisted, she wouldn't have been able to act on her desires. It took only one of you to be strong enough to stop."

Gabe put his head in his hands and groaned. When he lifted his eyes, Stevens was staring at him, this time with compassion.

"I'm disappointed, Gabe, but didn't I tell you about my gambling problem the other night?" he said. "None of us is perfect. We simply can't be. So I'm upset, but I'm not judging you. I just want you to think about whether living for nothing but yourself, by your own rules, is worth all of this."

Stevens slapped Gabe's back gently. He turned and walked toward the orphanage.

"Good night, man," he said. "I'm praying for you."

Gabe sat there in the dark and in the silence, fully seeing himself for the first time. His seasons of accomplishment flashed before his mind's eye: his marriage to Rachelle, the professional accolades and awards, the birth of his children, his complacency with everything. The arrogance and sense of entitlement. The thrill he thought an affair would bring. The emptiness that followed. The joy of helping a Ugandan woman who had been bedridden for months feel better. The despair over possibly returning home the same as he had left.

He just couldn't. He sat there and sobbed and replayed those scenes over and over. And for the first time with pure sincerity, he called out to God.

"I need you now, Lord. I don't know any other way."

32

Rachelle turned on the cell and listened to Gabe's messages with disgust.

He had been calling off and on for two days now, and she hadn't bothered to respond. He hadn't mentioned Veronica, so she was curious to know if he was aware that this nurse and girlfriend had contacted her.

Then again, knowing Gabe, he was playing innocent. He'd take whatever position served him best. Since the "don't ask, don't tell" policy had been working, he wasn't going to alter it.

Rachelle still didn't know if she loved him or whether that should factor into her decisions about the future. Had that mattered when she married him?

She had reached the conclusion that whatever happened to their relationship long term, they were going to have to develop better communication and some level of respect, for the sake of their children. She also realized that whatever doubts she had about her marriage, something was there, because when she allowed Veronica's news flash to penentrate her defenses, it hurt deeply to imagine that Gabe had slept with another woman, and one she knew at that.

How would Mom tell me to handle this?

Rachelle smirked. She could hear her mother now—"What do you mean, what should you do? He's a heart surgeon. Go shopping and get over it!"

And Alanna?

That one was trickier. Little sis seemed to be mellowing, so Rachelle wasn't sure what she could expect—advice to forgive and try to work things out with Gabe, or an itinerary on when and where the beat-downs for Veronica and Gabe should occur.

Rachelle was leaning toward the latter, but she was pretty sure that wouldn't make God happy, and she was glad that Aunt Irene, who sat in the passenger seat perusing a magazine, couldn't read her mind.

She drove into the parking lot in front of Cynthia Bridgeforth's medical office while she listened to Gabe's fifth and final message.

"Rachelle," he paused for a few seconds and sighed. "I'm calling to say I'm sorry. For everything. We have a lot to work through when I get home, but I want you to know that I'm ready to try. No more games."

That was a first. Rachelle pulled the phone away from her ear, as if it were contagious.

Aunt Irene looked at her. "What?"

Rachelle shook her head. "Gabe left me a thoughtful message. I'm not sure what's going on, but he sounded different."

Aunt Irene smiled. "That's a good thing," she said. "Maybe he'll come home to a different wife."

Rachelle tucked the phone away without responding.

Maybe he would, and maybe he wouldn't. She had thought about all that Aunt Irene had advised her a few days ago and all that Aunt Melba had shared last week.

Aunt Melba was right about Troy—Rachelle was playing with

193

fire. And she was right about the need for Rachelle to stop living on someone else's coattails. Rachelle couldn't thrive and be the "daughter of," "wife of," "mother of," forever.

Still, she was scared. Changing might mean losing the life she knew. She wasn't sure she was ready to stop being Mrs. Covington, just for the sake of being more self-aware. She also wasn't sure she could keep turning a blind eye to her husband's transgressions, especially when they slapped her in the face.

"What are you so lost in thought about?" Aunt Irene asked.

Rachelle shrugged. "Everything, I guess." She grabbed her purse and stepped out of the car. "Come on, let's go in."

Rachelle held open the door to Dr. Cynthia's office and leaned against it, giving Aunt Irene plenty of time to enter with the assistance of her walker.

"This is a shame," Aunt Irene said. "I look like a ninety-year-old woman!"

Cynthia was standing just inside the pediatric office, waiting to greet her.

"Oh hush! You don't look a day over fifty," she told Aunt Irene and gave her a hug.

Rachelle thought that was pushing it, but given that Aunt Irene was actually sixty, it was a compliment.

"Come on in and get comfortable," Cynthia said.

They had agreed that Aunt Irene would spend two hours in the waiting room, greeting children and their parents when they arrived and offering to read books to the younger ones, if they were interested. Cynthia had positioned a straight-back chair for Aunt Irene near a small table that was stacked with a variety of books.

"The kids will probably come over to the table and tell you what they'd like to read," Cynthia said. "Just play it by ear, and have fun, Irene."

Aunt Irene smiled. Rachelle could tell she was nervous but determined to give it a try.

The cozy waiting room bustled with busy toddlers and tired mothers. Some were yelling at babies who could walk but weren't yet able to articulate their thoughts. Some mothers seemed overwhelmed by several children they were trying to keep in line.

After observing for a few minutes, Rachelle asked the receptionist for the other volunteer smock and began rounding up the kids to steer them in Aunt Irene's direction.

"Come on, sweetie," she said with a smile to one busy little girl who was sucking her thumb and a lollipop at the same time. "Let's read a book."

The girl's mother seemed baffled by the invitation.

"I'm going to take her over to the table so that nice lady sitting over there can read a story to her," Rachelle told the woman. "Is that okay?"

The mother nodded cautiously and watched to see what her daughter would do. The girl, who was about three, took a seat at the table and squirmed until Aunt Irene began reading and pointing to the book's colorful pictures.

"Where is the red ball?" she asked.

Before the girl could answer, a boy who was sitting nearby with his mother piped up. "Right there!" he yelled. "The dog has the ball in his mouth!"

The boy's mother laughed. "I didn't know you were even listening," she told him. "Go to the table so she can read to you."

Rachelle marveled at how quickly most of the kids became engaged as Aunt Irene raised and lowered her voice and made animal and car engine sounds to match the action and dialogue on each page.

About an hour into the session, Aunt Irene had read four books and was now sitting in a chair near the waiting room bookshelf, organizing the titles. She pulled out books that were torn or covered with teeth marks and put the others in alphabetical order.

"I know it won't look like this for long, once the kids start searching for what they want," she told Rachelle, "but for now, it makes me feel better."

When a fresh round of youngsters filled the waiting room, Aunt Irene started the process over.

The door leading to the exam room opened and instead of a nurse emerging to call for the next patient, Cynthia stuck her head out and motioned for Rachelle to join her.

"Melba told me you want to volunteer too," she said. "Come back here with me."

Rachelle tried to appear unfazed, but she was thrilled. "I'll be back, Auntie," she told Irene.

She followed Cynthia down a short, brightly colored hallway, into a mid-sized room. Rachelle grinned when she saw the chart with letters on the wall, diminishing in size from top to bottom.

"I get to help administer eye exams?"

Cynthia nodded. "If you don't mind. You're still licensed, right? The nurse will bring the patients who need one back to you."

"Sure," Rachelle said. "I haven't done this in forever, but I'll give it a try."

Cynthia smiled. "It'll come back to you," she said and stepped out of the room. She returned seconds later with a white lab coat and held out her hand to Rachelle. "Give me that volunteer smock, and you take this."

Rachelle chuckled and complied. She positioned herself on the stool behind the piece of equipment she would look through to peer into a child's pupils and waited for a nurse to bring a young patient her way.

She looked around the room—at the seaside mural that featured dolphins flying through the air, catching letters of the alphabet—and smiled. An excitement she hadn't felt for a long time swelled inside of her. She was about to contribute something, and it felt really, really good.

33

*R*achelle had downplayed the encounter with Troy for as long as she could, but today, she realized she had to stop running.

Troy had called her again a few times at Aunt Irene's and tried to apologize, but she had rushed him off the phone.

"It's no big deal, Troy. Forget about it, okay?" The last time he had called, Rachelle hung up before he could respond.

He followed up by mailing a card and writing a brief note.

It is a big deal. We need to talk. Until we do, this won't ever be resolved, for either of us.

He included his email address and cell phone number and asked her to give him a date and time when they could sit down together, with Pastor Taylor or someone of her choosing. Rachelle responded by putting the information in File 13.

Today he was trying a new tactic. How had he gotten her cell phone number?

"I hope you don't feel like you're being stalked, Rachelle," he said. "We just really need to talk. I need to apologize for my recent behavior and see where we stand. I'll be at the church all day today. If you stop by, Pastor Taylor has agreed to sit and listen, or sit and talk with us. Whatever we need. He's my mentor as well as my boss, and I trust him. You can bring someone with you if you feel like you need some support. Just come, Rachelle. Please."

She sighed. This sounded too much like marriage counseling, and she was no longer his wife.

Yet even Alanna was taking his side. "Talk to the man, Chelle! You've got to clear up whatever there is between you two."

Rachelle pulled in front of Hair Pizzazz and tucked the phone in her purse. She was Aunt Melba's first client of the day.

"Why you needed to come in at seven a.m. when all you're doing is driving 'Miss Daisy' to volunteer at Cynthia's clinic is beyond me," Aunt Melba teased. "My next client doesn't come in until ten thirty today, so I got out of bed early for you."

Rachelle smiled. "Well, thank you. 'Miss Daisy' is excited about reading to the kids at the clinic. She likes to get there when Cynthia opens. I happen to like it a lot too. I've been helping with eye exams."

Aunt Melba lowered Rachelle's head into the shampoo bowl and nodded. "Cynthia told me. She says you're great with the kids and the parents."

Rachelle was beginning to think so too. Since they were alone, however, she had a more pressing matter on her mind. "Troy keeps trying to contact me. Can you believe it, Aunt Melba?"

Melba was quiet as she worked shampoo through Rachelle's hair and scrubbed her scalp. "What does he want, Rachelle?" she finally asked.

"He keeps apologizing for kissing me and says he wants to meet so we can put this behind us."

Melba stood back and looked at her. "I actually think that's a good idea, under the right circumstances. Both of you need to deal with what happened so you can bless and release each other. You need to move on so you can get things straight with Gabe.

And it hasn't escaped my attention that this fine man is walking around Jubilant unattended. If I were about thirty years younger, I'd be telling him to kick you to the curb once and for all."

Rachelle raised her head and tried to keep from leaking water onto the floor. "Aunt Melba!"

"I'm serious," she said. "You don't need to be looking at him, but I can!"

Rachelle resumed her position and shook her head in exasperation.

"Seriously though, Rachelle, you need to talk and get this resolved," Melba said. "It's probably weighing on him because he works at church, with Pastor Taylor, and he wants to make sure he's doing the right things before God."

Rachelle hadn't considered that. Maybe Troy was trying to clear this up so he could minister more effectively through the music. If that was the case, she had been hampering him.

She told Melba about his plea for her to come to the church today and his offer for her to bring someone along. "Will you go with me?"

Melba glanced at the clock. It was 7:20 a.m. "I'll be done with your hair in another hour, but I don't want to miss my next client."

Rachelle frowned. "Didn't you just tell me she won't be in until ten thirty?"

Aunt Melba nodded. "Yep, but this could take awhile. Call him and ask if he and Pastor Taylor mind coming here. If they get here right at eight thirty, that would give us almost two hours. I want to help."

Troy had left his cell phone number in the message. Rachelle listened to it again and stored the digits in her temporary memory bank.

He picked up on the first ring. "Thanks for calling me back." He sounded anxious.

"Would you and Pastor Taylor be able to meet me at Melba's salon in about an hour?"

Troy agreed without hesitating. "We'll be there. Thank you, Rachelle. I appreciate it."

She clicked off the phone and realized she was feeling uneasy. This could be the close of a difficult chapter for both of them, but first, some deep wounds might have to be reopened.

34

*G*abe couldn't believe it.

They were just children, many of them the same ages as Taryn and Tate, just eight and ten. But here they were, chanting rhythms and walking for miles and miles, for no reason at all but to remain safe, to keep from being kidnapped and forced to join a murderous army.

People called them night commuters, because that's what they did. They walked, sang, and prayed all night, hopeful that if they kept moving instead of sleeping in one of the displaced persons camps, they would stay out of harm's way. Some of their friends and relatives had been captured by the Lord's Resistance Army and tortured or raped. Some had been forced to become soldiers and kill people they knew and loved.

When some of those young victims managed to escape, they too joined the band of night wanderers. Staying alive and free from the army's grip was worth the wear and tear on their feet that came with the twelve-mile, one-way commute.

Gabe watched from the shadows and wanted to weep. His heart broke. *God, please help them.*

For the second time in days, he uttered a genuine prayer. For the first time ever, he received a reply in his heart.

That is what I have sent you to do.

When Stevens and a couple of Ugandan locals were preparing to slip away from the well-lit perimeter of the orphanage earlier this evening for a "special mission," Gabe had insisted on coming along. Stevens and Chrissa had tried to talk him out of it.

"Gabe, this is your first time on a mission trip. This can be dangerous. Just stay," Chrissa had said. She looked at her husband. "Lyle and I are prayed up; we're prepared for whatever may happen, but I'm not sure you have that same level of assurance right now. Northern Uganda is dangerous."

Gabe knew Chrissa was talking about the need to have a relationship with God. She didn't know about his desert experience, though. He had connected with God and was ready to be of service. If Stevens believed this mission to another part of the country warranted the risk, he was going too.

While they were en route, Stevens shared details about Joseph Kony's Lord's Resistance Army and about how, if children weren't rescued or hidden away, they could be taken and turned against their own families.

It happened every night, and youths whose parents had died of AIDS or in some other fashion were the most vulnerable.

"Malichi and Akello have already scoped out a couple of villages where children are living alone, fending for themselves," Stevens explained while he and Gabe crouched in the back of the a car so no one could see them. Stevens's white skin and Gabe's light complexion would make them easy targets.

Malichi and Akello scanned the streets to make sure no one was following them.

"We'll go into the villages and tell them to come with us, to safety," Stevens said. "Since I am white, they know I'm not part of LRA. They trust me when I tell them I'm taking them to a better place.

"We bring them to southern Uganda, to one of the orphanages that cares for children, and they remain there until they are able to care for themselves."

Now, under the veil of night, they had paused on their way to one of the designated villages near Acholiland to watch the night commuters' routine trek.

"If they are all walking, how can we be sure that the children we want to help are at home, in their villages?" Gabe asked.

"Not everyone walks," Stevens said. "Some are afraid; some just don't know yet. There are still many children to help. We do what we can."

Gabe sat back and looked at his friend. "How long have you been doing this, Stevens? Why haven't you told me about this?"

Stevens shrugged. "When we do things for Christ, he is the only one who needs to know. This is not about me doing 'good works.' It's about me loving others because I've been blessed to be loved."

Malichi pulled away from their hiding spot and drove to the village he had selected. When he gave Stevens a thumbs-up, Stevens put on a lightweight hooded jacket and hid his face as much as possible.

He and Akello trotted along the edge of the village and entered two thatched huts. Within minutes, they returned with three children.

They thrust them onto the backseat of the car, next to Gabe. The saucer-sized eyes of two little boys and a little girl, not more than four, peered up at him.

Stevens tumbled in with them, breathless but excited. He motioned for Malichi to take off.

The two boys huddled together on the seat. The girl climbed onto Gabe's lap and stuck her thumb in her mouth. She clung to his shirt as if they were on a tightrope and if she let go, she would spin into a freefall.

Gabe was speechless.

Akello turned toward the children and spoke to them in Acholi, their tribal language.

"I told them they are safe and they can go to sleep," he said as Malichi drove swiftly, racing through the cover of night to reach southern Uganda. "They know we are their caretakers until we get them to the orphanage. I told them we are good friends and that we will protect them, okay?"

Gabe nodded. Wait until he told Rachelle about this.

Then he realized he couldn't, not only because he couldn't risk the safety of these three youngsters and other children like them, but also because maybe it was too late for his marriage.

Yet the biblical passage that Stevens had shared with him just last night, before they set out on this adventure, had encouraged him.

With God, nothing is impossible.

Gabe stroked the cheek of the little girl who lay against his chest falling into a deeper sleep with each mile they crossed, and he knew.

It was time to go home. For good.

35

The years peeled away as Rachelle sat on Melba's red sofa, across from Troy.

She and Troy were twenty-one and twenty-two again, standing at the altar preparing to say "I do." She saw it as clearly as if it had happened yesterday. And yet, it had not.

Pastor Taylor and Aunt Melba abruptly reminded her of that. She and Troy were fifteen years older now and had become different people, living different lives. The only context in which they needed to view that November 9 wedding was one that allowed them to grieve for its potential and put it to rest.

Pastor Taylor and Aunt Melba agreed on those ground rules from the beginning.

"That just clears up why we're here," Pastor Taylor said. "There's no need to play games or be coy in the hopes that it will allow you to rekindle what you once had. That relationship died a long time ago, without a proper burial.

"I'm not saying you can turn your emotions on and off like a faucet—I know that's impossible," he said. "But your memories and feelings about this part of your past can't continue to shape your future. It's just not healthy."

He sat back and folded his arms. "Right now, I'm not Pastor

Taylor. I'm Malcolm—Troy's 'uncle,' here to listen and offer fair and equal support."

Aunt Melba nodded. "You know who I am. I've known you since your sophomore year of college, Troy. I'm here to listen and help both of you."

Pastor Taylor—Malcolm—looked at Rachelle. "You're married with two children. I don't know the status of your relationship with your husband, but the fact that you're here is a bit telling."

He turned to Troy. "You've been engaged twice and just went through the breakup of another serious relationship. I know you're tired of this happening."

Rachelle tried to mask her surprise. Troy had as much at stake as she did.

Pastor Taylor sighed and rested his hands on his miniature paunch. "Tell me what's going on."

With his laid-back demeanor and gentle smile, he seemed safe. Rachelle understood why Troy confided in him.

"I've been here for almost three weeks and nobody has addressed the fact that Troy was my first love—the love of my life," Rachelle said. "Everybody keeps telling me to get myself together and focus on my husband, without acknowledging that things weren't right in my second marriage from the start because of my feelings for Troy.

"Troy and I loved each other enough to get married, and even though everyone thought it was too soon and inappropriate to elope, for us it was right."

Troy leaned forward and made a teepee with his hands. "Then why did you leave me, Rachelle? And if you felt you had to, why didn't you tell me face-to-face?"

His voice was controlled, but she heard the thread of hurt coursing through the question. Rachelle felt it too.

She lowered her eyes. "I couldn't tell you face-to-face because, first of all, I knew I wouldn't be able to do it. One look in your eyes and I wouldn't have left."

Melba leaned over and touched her arm. "Look at Troy while you're talking to him now, Rachelle. Look him in the eyes."

That was the problem. She still couldn't bring herself to do that. She loved him too much to really tell him goodbye.

She considered the revelation about his relationship woes. This was about his healing as much as hers. She owed him all she could give.

Troy obviously saw her struggling. He took her hand in his. "I love you, Rachelle."

She looked at Aunt Melba for the usual warning and tried to pull away, but he wouldn't loosen his grasp. Melba didn't react.

"Let me finish," Troy said. "I loved you from the first time I saw you on Everson's campus, heading into the McPherson Hall choir room. When you opened your mouth and sang like an angel, I think my heart memorized your name. That won't ever change.

"We dated for three years and didn't make the decision to marry lightly," he said. "We got married during our senior year so we could find graduate programs that met both our needs, remember?"

Rachelle recalled the late nights they had spent mapping out their five-year plan after choir rehearsals, over homework, pizza, and tender kisses.

"We had it all figured out, didn't we?" she said, mindful that he continued to grasp her hand.

"What we had then was real," Troy said. He peered at her until she locked eyes with him. "And for one crazy moment last week, I thought it was *still* real."

Rachelle held her breath.

"But you and I both know that it's not," Troy said. "I am sorry I overstepped my bounds and kissed you. I was out of line and just plain wrong. I'm representing God before everyone I encounter—even you, and I apologize."

Rachelle didn't know what to say. She was the one who owed him an apology. More than one. She was the one who shattered their marriage and never told him why. She was the one who remarried, thinking she could forget what they had.

Pastor Taylor cleared his throat. "Was that all you wanted to say, Troy?"

He shook his head. "No, I guess not. This conversation has been a long time coming, and I really just need to get everything out.

"I told you I forgave you, Rachelle, and in my head, I did, a long time ago. But if you ask the two women I dated after grad school at Georgia Tech whether I was over you, they would beg to differ. So would the woman I asked to marry me just before I moved back to Jubilant."

Rachelle's eyes grew large. There was someone else? What was all this talk for, then?

Troy produced a slow smile. "I know you're wondering where that came from. But yes, I've dated and I've been in love with other people. I'm in love with someone now, but she doesn't believe that I love her as much or more than I loved you.

"She keeps telling me that you are the silent partner in our relationship, because I trust her just enough to love me, but not enough to let down my guard, in case she decides to leave too."

Rachelle felt the golf ball–sized lump in her throat expand into a grapefruit. "Troy, I am so sorry. I'm sorry for promising to spend my life with you and instead, leaving you a good-bye note next to your coffee cup. I'm sorry for putting my desire to please my parents before our marriage. They dangled the threat of not paying for me to go to optometry school if I didn't move on with my life without you, but I'm wise enough to know now that if I had wanted it badly enough, I would have found other ways to reach that goal."

Rachelle inhaled. *No tears today, please, God.* "I've never loved anyone as deeply as I loved you, Troy. Not even my husband, Gabe. And all these years, I think he's known it, so I owe him an apology too. After that kiss last week, I realized that we can't go back in time. We're different people. But I don't think that will ever keep me from loving you, or being in love with the man you were."

Pastor Taylor laid his hands on top of both of theirs, which were still locked together. "I'm hearing a lot of regret," he said. "Yes, it's too late to think that you two can pick up where you left off and spend your lives together, happily after ever. But it's not too late to acknowledge a never-ending affection for each other. You can feel strongly about someone and still decide to move on. If your decision honors God, he'll give you beauty, even for those ashes."

As Pastor Taylor gave their hands a squeeze and leaned back, Rachelle slipped her hand out of Troy's.

She accepted his answer. However, the unspoken question was, what would it mean if they didn't want to move on? What if they did want to try again? Why was everyone so adamant that they shouldn't?

Rachelle wanted those answers, even though she didn't deserve them.

She saw something she didn't quite understand in Troy's eyes too. He looked from her to Melba to Pastor Taylor.

"I've been living in the land of what-if for years," he said. "What if Rachelle found me and wanted to try again? What if she was still single and we could pick up where we left off? What if our love was strong enough to overcome any challenges that our reunion might cause the people around us? Those are legitimate questions, aren't they?"

Aunt Melba pursed her lips. "He's right, Pastor Taylor. People ask those questions every single day and decide that finding answers is worth risking everything else. Usually the odds are stacked against them, but that can't always be the case."

She turned her attention to Troy and Rachelle.

"When those questions arise, I think you need to not only look at just the Troy and Rachelle equation," Aunt Melba said. "Look at the panorama of your lives. Everything—from your service to God to your careers to your hobbies to your extended family to your long-term life vision. In the entire scheme of things, ask yourself where a relationship between you two would fit."

She sat back on the sofa and shook her head. "I don't know that either of you have ready answers to those broad questions today."

Rachelle leaned forward. "Melba's right, Troy—my feelings for you can't rule my entire life. I'm not prepared to put everything on hold like I've been fantasizing about doing.

"But I am prepared to tell you that you did absolutely nothing wrong. You were a good husband and you are a good man. You loved me and treated me like I was your queen. I was just plain stupid to leave you. But I did, and I have to live with that.

"When we got married, I was a baby in a grown woman's body. I allowed my parents to orchestrate my every move, and I'm still dealing with issues of control with them that I need to address. And all these years later, I've realized that I still don't really know who I am or what I want out of life. I need to figure that out before I do anything else."

Troy sat back in his chair and folded his arms, oblivious to the

211

tears that now streamed down his face. "So that's it, Rachelle? You left me on a whim because your mommy and daddy said so? My mother was just a seamstress and my Rolling Stone daddy was a bus driver, so I wasn't good enough. That's the answer I've been longing for all these years? You should have just put that in your farewell note."

They sat in silence and let those words simmer.

"Don't beat yourself up," Pastor Taylor told Rachelle. "You'd be surprised at how many people go through life making choices based on someone else's likes and dislikes or because someone else is footing the bill."

Rachelle looked at him. He must think she was awful.

Pastor Taylor shook his head. "I see it every day, from the pulpit to the pew. No one is immune. The interesting thing is that God brought both of you back to Jubilant this summer to revisit this."

He looked at Troy. "You took a job here, in the place where you had your heart broken, for a reason. Something led you here, before you even knew Rachelle was coming for an extended visit. What was it?"

Troy shrugged. "When they called and told me about the engineering department fellowship, I saw it as a great opportunity for me and a good place to raise Chaundra. You were here and there was an opening at the church, so that was the icing on the cake. I prayed about it and told God that if this wasn't for me, to close the door. Instead, he opened it wide."

Pastor Taylor turned to Rachelle. She looked at Troy.

"I haven't mentioned this, but Jillian is dying," she said softly. She gave Troy a moment to absorb the news.

"I learned about a month ago that she has terminal cancer, and in dealing with that news, I just . . . flipped. This other side of me tried to break free. On the morning my plane landed in Houston after a visit with Jillian, instead of going home to my so-called fabulous life, I directed the car here, to the one place I remembered being truly happy, other than when I gave birth to my children. That's why I'm here. I guess I was chasing happiness, and it just so happened that the biggest part of that—you, Troy—wound up being here to meet me."

Pastor Taylor looked from one to the other. "So what are you two going to do now?" he asked. "Your feelings for each other aren't going to dissipate like smoke. How are you going to handle that?"

Rachelle and Troy stared at each other for the longest time, as if they were mustering the courage to get it over with.

"I want you to be happy, Troy," Rachelle said. "I'll always love you, and I'll always wish the best for you."

Troy held her gaze and gave her a half smile. "Here I am, a grown man who still gets weak-kneed in your presence. And yet, I know I'm in love with who you were, because I don't really know you now. Thank you for telling me what happened; I've wondered all these years what I could have done differently. I'll always love you too."

He gathered Rachelle in his arms. She rested her head on his shoulder and closed her eyes. His embrace felt good, but for the first time in forever, she realized she didn't belong there.

36

*R*achelle's eyes flew open and she clutched her throat. She sat up in bed and wiped sweat from her brow. A single word came to her.

Pray.

She frowned.

Her? Pray? For who? For what?

Jillian.

She struggled to fight off panic. She wanted to get up and run downstairs to the living room, where Aunt Irene lay resting. She would know what to say.

Or maybe Uncle Charles could help her—he was a deacon in the church. She had heard him render some moving prayers from the altar at St. Peter's Baptist.

What did she know, except the prayers she had recited on occasion as a child?

Now I lay me down to sleep, I pray the Lord my soul to keep . . .

Then there were the ones she bowed to nearly two decades ago, during her choir days in college. Watching her fellow choir members pray with such passion and faith had been awe-inspiring. She had been curious about what that felt like, but had never sought an answer. Life had been pretty good without extra rules and commandments.

This morning, though, something or someone was summoning her to speak, and for the first time in a long time, she believed it was God. He had put Jillian on her heart and mind, and knowing her friend's circumstances, she was willing to help however she could.

Rachelle slowly climbed out of Reuben's bed and knelt against it, on her knees. She bowed her head and cupped her hands in front of her.

"God," she said in a whisper. "You haven't heard from me in a long, long time, but I think you just woke me up. For Jillian, my sister-friend. Seems like you and she have a wonderful friendship, and even though you'll be taking her away from this earth soon, she's satisfied with the love you've shown her. I don't know where she is in that process or what her needs are this morning, but God, I ask that you grant her the peace and comfort that you are able to provide. Let her still be happy, God, and trusting you to do what's best. Amen."

Rachelle remained in that position for several more minutes and let the tears fall. Somehow, she knew God had heard and answered. She felt a calm wash over her that she had never before experienced.

She recalled the prayer she had uttered just weeks earlier, when she lay across the bed in the Hotel Magnolia and begged God to give her a sign that he existed.

In the wee hours of this day, he had, and to her surprise, she welcomed his presence.

37

$\mathscr{R}$achelle poured her third cup of tea and sat at the kitchen table alone, twiddling her thumbs and watching the red lights of the digital clock like a hawk.

When it was officially 10 a.m. Central Time and 8 a.m. Pacific, she called San Diego.

Patrick, Jillian's husband, picked up on the second ring. "Good morning, Rachelle. How did you know to call?" he asked. Obviously he had caller ID.

Rachelle gripped the phone tighter.

Please, God, no . . .

Patrick understood the silence and quickly reassured her. "No, it's not that, Rachelle," he said. "Jillian's still with us. But she has been in a lot of pain because she's refusing to take regular doses of her medication. She wants to be as lucid as possible these last few weeks. She reminisced all day yesterday about the things you guys did together over the years. Your call is going to thrill her."

Rachelle was simultaneously heartened and saddened. She hated to think of her beautiful friend suffering so much. "Does she feel up to talking, Patrick?"

"Oh yeah," he said. "She consumes enough medicine to take the edge off the pain, to get to what she calls her 'good zone.' That allows her to function during the day. The pain comes back full force just around nightfall, and she'll go ahead and fully medicate then, for the evening. She's right here, Rachelle. Let me give her the phone."

Rachelle sighed with relief.

"Is this you, Rae? I must have 'prayed you up,'" Jillian said. Despite her weak voice, Rachelle heard the same Jillian she'd always known.

"Yep, my friend, that's exactly what you did," Rachelle said. "When I woke up this morning, you were the first thing on my mind, so I climbed out of bed and talked to God about you."

She knew Jillian was smiling.

"I'm really glad to hear that, Rae. Thank you."

"I'm glad to have a chance to talk to you," Rachelle said. "I've wanted to touch base since the party, but I wasn't sure if you were up to taking calls.

"I've been thinking about you a lot, Jill. People say stuff like this all the time, but I want you to know that your strength and faith during this time have shown me what it means to really live."

There. Rachelle had said what she'd been feeling all this time since Jillian's invitation had arrived in the mail. She was in a challenging place right now, trying to figure it all out, but it was a good place, because after her experience this morning, she knew God cared about her too.

"You don't know how much that means to me, Rae," Jillian said. Her voice was growing weaker. "Others who came to the party have said the same thing. But you and I have been estranged for a long time. I should have never told you not to marry Gabe. I was out of line. It was your choice."

Rachelle gazed out of the window and shook her head, as if Jillian could see her through the phone. "Don't apologize, especially

217

since you were right," she finally said. "He was and is arrogant, he was and is controlling, and he was and is in need of a trophy wife rather than an equal partner. Up until now, I could live with all of that. Now, I just don't know."

"What does that mean? Are you and Gabe still together?" Jillian asked.

"Yes, we are," Rachelle said. "But I've been struggling with whether to stay. I know I married him for security, although I hadn't gotten over Troy. I loved Troy, Jillian, and I'm not so sure that I still don't. Do you believe in second chances?"

The silence extended for so long that Rachelle feared they had either been disconnected or her friend had fallen asleep. But Jillian finally responded.

"Second, and even third chances can and do happen, Rachelle," Jillian said, "but not at the expense of something God has already ordained and blessed. When you married Gabe, that became the man you should honor. Unless he has been abusive or in some other way broken your marriage vows, you can't just decide to rewind life and try to start over again—fifteen years later—with the man you first loved. Life doesn't work that way. God wants you to be happy, but he also wants you to keep your commitments."

Rachelle's heart sank with the realization that her friend wasn't giving her an easy way out. It appeared that Gabe had committed adultery, but had she been an accomplice by not calling him on it? She had more questions, if Jillian had enough strength to keep talking.

"Can I ask you something else?"

"Anything," Jillian said. "I don't know how much more time I have left, Rae, so let's talk. I want this conversation to matter, forever. What do you want to know?"

"How did you connect with God?" Rachelle asked, almost afraid that the answer would be so amazing that she couldn't possibly accomplish a similar feat.

She rose from her seat to check the pots on the stove. She was making spaghetti sauce for lunch and wanted to make sure nothing was in danger of burning. After a quick perusal, she repositioned herself at the table, thankful that she hadn't been interrupted by one of the girls or Aunt Irene. She wanted to hear Jillian's response without distractions.

"I traveled all over the world taking pictures and saw some of the most amazing sights and some of the most horrific," Jillian said. "Witnessing both ends of life's spectrum led me to question how this world was really fashioned and what purpose all of us play in it.

"When I went to Jerusalem about eight years ago, seeing the historic places mentioned in the Bible and seeing the people who live in that region fervently praying several times a day, despite whatever else was going on, just changed me." Jillian paused and coughed. "I realized that for them, everything began and ended with a reverence for God. I wanted to be connected to something more meaningful and lasting than my pictures.

"When I began exploring Christianity and found a church here in San Diego that taught me how to read the Bible and relate it to my own experience, I finally got a sense of who God is and how we all fit into the world's vast landscape."

Rachelle couldn't help but interrupt. She needed to know too. "Where *do* we fit?"

"In the palm of God's hand, Rae. It sounds simplistic, but it serves as the foundation of everything—particularly how we live and how we love," Jillian said. "You know how much I struggled at one point with being part Asian and part black; but when I began to rest in God, I understood that he loves all of us, despite our cultural, racial, or personality differences. That meant I could love myself unconditionally because I was one of his children. He wants every one of us to love each other the same way."

Rachelle frowned. All it boiled down to was love?

The strain that had permeated Jillian's voice had disappeared. "It's hard to articulate, Rae, but it's like I was a deflated balloon until God blew his breath into me. I've never been the same since. He sustains me, he makes me laugh, he loves me—good, bad, ugly; even when I'm passing gas from this medicine."

"What?!" Rachelle laughed out loud.

Leave it to Jillian to lighten the mood, even while discussing something as serious as her faith.

"Studying the Bible and connecting with others who understand and appreciate God's love has helped me deepen my relationship with him," Jillian said. "When I got the news about how much time I supposedly have left, I was devastated.

"Patrick and I had begun trying to have a baby. I had a lot more living to do! But if God wants me to come home, overstaying my welcome here on earth would lead to more heartache than I probably could handle on my own."

Jillian sighed, and Rachelle could tell that she was weeping.

"I don't know the reason he's shortening my stay—I can only speculate. But I do know that I love him and trust him, no matter what he decides. And I'm grateful for the ride I've had."

"How do I get to that place with him?" Rachelle wiped her wet eyes with the back of her hand. "I'm embarrassed to tell you that I can't even figure out who I am or what I want out of life. That Top Ten List you asked all of us to create? I have one thing on my list, Jill, and it's not even a real goal. I am pitiful. How do I get happy?"

Rachelle felt ashamed for seeking her dying friend's advice on how to live.

"Accept how much God loves you, honey, and run toward him instead of in the opposite direction," Jillian said. "When you anchor your heart in his love, it can't help but flow outward. God will begin showing you your purpose, when you're ready to walk in it."

Rachelle finally believed she was.

38

The courtroom was nearly empty, and for that, Rachelle was thankful.

A blond man carrying a slim notepad entered and slid into a seat on the second row to the right. The *Jubilant Herald* had remembered to send a reporter. Great.

She sat across the aisle from him and tried to shield the girls from his view. Yasmin was next to her, followed by Indigo, then Uncle Charles. Her dad, who had flown in from Philadelphia last night to support his sister, sat next to Uncle Charles. Aunt Melba, Cynthia, and Pastor Taylor sat on the row behind them.

Rachelle couldn't recall ever praying for anything or anyone as fervently as she had prayed for Aunt Irene over the past twenty-four hours. Her aunt was a good and loving person who needed help, not a devastating punishment. Rachelle's conversations with God were too new for her to know exactly what to say, but she trusted that the Psalms she had been reading with Aunt Irene were an accurate barometer of what he found acceptable. She felt hopeful that her pleas of God, grant her mercy, had been heard. Between the family's collective and personal prayers, Rachelle had to trust that everything would turn out okay.

Everyone stood when Judge Candice Carmichael entered the

courtroom. She took Aunt Irene's case file from the court clerk and skimmed its contents.

"Mrs. Burns, I was prepared to simply record the charges against you today and schedule a trial date, but am I correct in understanding that you are ready to enter a plea this morning?"

Aunt Irene glanced at her lawyer and nodded.

"I need you to speak, rather than use head motions, for the benefit of the clerk transcribing these proceedings," Judge Carmichael told her.

"I'm sorry, Your Honor," Aunt Irene said softly. "Yes, I am entering an Alford plea."

Her attorney, John Dupree, had explained to the family last night that by making this kind of plea, Aunt Irene was not technically pleading guilty, in the traditional sense. Instead, she was acknowledging that there was enough evidence to find her guilty of causing bodily harm to another person while driving drunk.

The Alford plea allowed her to take responsibility for her actions without assuming the guilt of someone who had committed the crime intentionally, and it allowed the prosecuting attorney to recommend a sentence that better fit her crime.

If this option hadn't been available, Aunt Irene informed the family that she would have entered a traditional guilty plea without qualms.

"I'm not trying to dodge the consequences of my actions," she had insisted, with her eyes fixed on Yasmin and Indigo. "I've taught you two, and your brother Reuben, to never do that, and I can't break my own rules."

As she stood before the judge this morning, the prosecutor summarized the details of the car accident and provided the judge with documentation of Aunt Irene's blood alcohol level.

Copies of the injured child's medical records were also entered into evidence.

"Judge, not only was she intoxicated with alcohol, blood tests revealed that she also had prescription pain medicine in her system," Kirby Branson said. "The worst part was that this accident resulted in more harm than just a few banged-up cars. Because of her negligence, a young boy will spend most of his summer in leg and arm casts."

John Dupree spoke on Aunt Irene's behalf.

"Mrs. Burns is an upstanding citizen, a retired schoolteacher, who coped with the grief of losing her only child by self-medicating in an unwise fashion. A fairly recent hip injury that required her to take several prescription medicines only compounded the issue.

"She is very remorseful, and recently began making a positive contribution to the lives of children about the age of the boy who was hurt in the accident. She is reading to youths in a local pediatric office and is prepared to continue this community service long term."

John held a document in the air. "I have a notarized statement about her excellent service from the doctor who operates the reading program."

Judge Carmichael nodded and turned toward Aunt Irene. "What do you have to say for yourself, Mrs. Burns?"

Aunt Irene had taken a seat while the lawyers presented the evidence. John helped her stand again so she could respond. She glanced at her family before speaking. "I don't know what to say, Your Honor, except that I am very sorry."

She began softly, but the longer she talked, the louder and more confident she grew. "I know you get apologies all day long, but I am truly horrified by what happened. I have asked my family to forgive me and also the little boy who I hurt, and his family. I wrote them a letter last week and my lawyer gave it to Mr. Branson to deliver. I love children, Your Honor. I would never have put that young man or his family in harm's way if I had been coherent.

"That's no excuse—I'm owning up to my failure. I started drinking years ago, after my son and his wife were killed in a car accident. My daughter-in-law's mother was deceased and her father was legally blind, so that meant my husband and I had to take custody of our three grandchildren.

"I can honestly say it has been a joy." Aunt Irene's voice began to tremble, but she continued. "They are beautiful young people, and they deserve much better than they've had from me when my drinking has spiraled out of control.

"I'm asking you to please give me a chance to right the things I've done wrong. They've already lost their biological parents. Please let me stay with them and make it up to them."

Before she finished speaking, a young couple entered the courtroom and sat on the last row of seats. Rachelle didn't recognize them, but they seemed to be hanging on to Aunt Irene's every word.

Rachelle ignored the knot forming in her stomach and turned her attention back to Judge Carmichael who was reviewing the sentence both parties had agreed upon, to decide whether she would approve it.

Please, God, grant her mercy, Rachelle prayed again.

"First of all, Mrs. Burns, let me commend you for taking care of your grandchildren after your devastating loss," the judge said. "I'm sure the experience has been rewarding for you and for them.

"However, I can't ignore the seriousness of this crime. You were driving drunk." She paused and let those words resonate. "Your actions injured a child and could have killed someone."

She paused again and stared at Aunt Irene, who didn't avert her gaze.

"I am taking into account the fact that you are a first offender, and that you've already begun giving back to the community by reading to pediatric patients. I will honor the guidelines set forth in this plea agreement and sentence you to one year of probation and 200 hours of community service, and I order you to complete an accredited substance abuse program, such as Alcoholics Anonymous." Judge Carmichael's expression was as nonchalant as if she were ordering a cup of coffee, but her warning pricked Rachelle's heart. "If you wind up back in here, Mrs. Burns, I'll revoke your license and you will serve time in jail. I hear stories like yours all the time—it's up to you to turn things around for these children you say you love."

"Thank you, Your Honor," Aunt Irene said. "I'll work hard to insure that I'm never in this position again."

Rachelle glanced at her cousins and saw that Indigo was weeping. Yasmin was too young to understand what the judge's orders meant, and she peered at Rachelle expectantly.

"Does this mean Mommy's not in trouble anymore?' "

"It means that she will make up for what happened by continuing to visit Dr. Bridgeforth's office to read books to children," Rachelle whispered. "It also means she will have to talk to someone about finding good ways to handle pain when her hips bother her. But she's had her surgery now; she'll be feeling a lot better in a few more months."

"So she's not going to jail?"

Yasmin covered her mouth to stifle a scream when Rachelle told her no.

Minutes later, outside the courtroom, Uncle Charles refused to give the *Herald* reporter a comment, and the man reluctantly left to file his story.

The family took turns hugging Aunt Irene, who was in tears. Rachelle noticed when she stepped aside that the couple who had listened to Aunt Irene's plea and sentence stood nearby, watching. Glaring. They had to be the parents of the little boy who was injured in the crash, she decided. The woman followed Aunt Irene's every move with her eyes.

When she noticed Rachelle staring, she challenged her. "What you looking at? I'm checking out the criminal who hurt my baby and just got off scot free, 'cause she said she was sorry."

Everyone froze in unison.

Where was the bailiff? Rachelle couldn't believe he had disappeared so quickly.

Her father stepped in front of Irene. "Ma'am, maybe you'd better leave," he said calmly.

The man who had accompanied the angry lady tugged at her arm. "That's alright, Angela," he said, while keeping his eyes on Rachelle's dad. "We don't want no trouble. These folks uppity. You see that. They bought that old lady's freedom. They gone pay for our son's doctor bills, though. That prosecutor told us so."

The woman yanked her arm free, and Herbert moved again to protect his sister.

But Aunt Irene gripped her walker and poked her head around him. "No, it's okay, Herb," she said. "I want to talk to her, if she'll let me."

"I'm listening." The woman flung her shoulder-length reddish-blond braids over her shoulder, pursed her full lips, and folded her thick arms. A deep frown creased her cinnamon brow, but even so, Rachelle was struck by her pretty features, which under different circumstances would have seemed friendly and inviting.

227

Aunt Irene shuffled toward the woman and her companion, with Uncle Charles at her side.

When she reached them, she sighed and pushed herself as upright as she could. "I'm glad you came today," she said softly.

Surprise registered on the man's face. "My wife and I are angry at you. We don't have much in this world, but your selfishness coulda taken our baby's life. He's all we got, and it took us years to have him. You coulda killed him."

Tears swam in Aunt Irene's eyes. "You two love your son and God, don't you?"

Now the woman's expression changed.

"How do I know?" Aunt Irene answered the woman's unasked question with a halfhearted smile. "Because there's nothing else keeping either of you from cursing my name right now. You're being way too kind for what I did."

The man looked at his wife. The fire in her eyes seemed to dim, but she didn't alter her stance.

"We received your letter," the man said, "but we had to come here today. My wife couldn't make peace with this until she heard what you had to say. She wanted to see you and hear you before she'd ask God to forgive you. We're here today really for her, to help her move on."

Aunt Irene peered into the woman's eyes. Even from where she stood, Rachelle could see the challenge the woman was issuing. Whatever Aunt Irene said had better be good.

"Nothing I can say to you right now will change how furious you must be at me for the pain I've caused and for the fear I put in your heart on the day of the accident," she began. "You heard me in courtroom—I lost a child of my own. I wouldn't wish that anguish on my worst enemy.

"I'm really sorry for hurting you and your baby with my selfish actions," Aunt Irene said. "What I did was wrong. If I had not been drinking and driving, your child wouldn't have a cast on his arm and leg, and he wouldn't have had to suffer pain and fear, and who knows what else. I am so very sorry, and I hope that someday, you and your baby can forgive me."

"Talk is cheap, you know," the mother said. "I hope you really meant what you told the judge, that you'll get some help. Next time around you won't be so lucky."

"I meant it, and with God's help, I will honor that promise," Aunt Irene said "I can also promise you that I won't ever forget what I've done, or this conversation. My husband and I have already talked to our insurance company. They haven't told us yet how they plan to handle the claim you've filed, but we've told them that we don't want to battle you. If whatever is settled on is fair, it's fair."

Rachelle recognized the wariness that filled the father's face. It had draped her own often enough in her exchanges with her husband.

"Thank you. That means a lot," he said. "My wife may not be able to forgive you today, and I don't know that I can either, but we got a place to start. And we don't want your money—we want you to keep your word. Don't wind up here again, hurting somebody else."

His response left Aunt Irene reeling.

Rachelle approached her quickly and began steering her away, back to the family, before Aunt Irene lost her composure.

The man pulled his wife away and rubbed her shoulders as they walked down the narrow corridor, toward the courthouse exit.

Before they turned a corner that led to an escalator, the mother paused and called out to Aunt Irene. "I can't do it today, but I'm going to pray about forgiving you. Please, just do what you said. I gave my son your letter, and I want to believe it's the truth."

With that, they were gone.

Aunt Irene turned to Rachelle and wept in her arms.

"Thank you, God," she uttered softly, when her tears finally abated. "You gave me a chance to ask for forgiveness and to help that family heal. Thank you, God."

The family filed quietly out of the courthouse behind Aunt Irene and Uncle Charles. Rachelle's heart was full of questions and emotions.

She didn't know what to make of what had transpired this morning—in the courtroom or afterward. She marveled at how graciously her aunt had handled her sentence and her encounter with her victims.

If this was what growing in God's grace could achieve, she needed to pick up her pace.

39

*D*addy was flying home tonight, just two days after his arrival, and Rachelle was glad they had this brief time alone.

She needed to talk with someone about the volcano churning inside of her, from questions about her husband's supposed infidelity to her unresolved anger at the role her parents played in the death of her marriage to Troy.

This evening, over dessert at a local café, Rachelle tried to keep it real. Over the summer, she had grown impatient with social niceties that only served to maintain artificial boundaries and relationships. She was realizing that only the truth allowed a person to have deep and authentic connections.

Life was messy—Aunt Irene's situation had proven that. But in taking responsibility for her actions, her aunt had opened the door for healing with her family and with her victim's parents, and she had made peace with the fact that she couldn't recover by herself. She needed help.

So did Rachelle, especially from her father.

She told him about her visit with Jillian and her struggle since that time to sort things out.

"So you're having an early life crisis?" he asked, sounding very much like Gabe.

Rachelle sighed. "Call it what you want, Daddy. Maybe I'm finally facing the truth about myself and about the way I've lived my life—mostly to please others, including you and Mom."

Herbert's eyes widened. "Where's all this coming from?"

She shrugged. "I won't get into all of it tonight, but I'm wrestling with a lot of things, Daddy. I'm angry at how my marriage to Troy ended, and I feel like I was pressured into leaving him by you and Mom. That wasn't right."

He sat back in his wooden seat and folded his arms. Rachelle could tell he wasn't angry, just surprised.

"Okay. Why is this the first time I'm hearing this?"

"Because I've never had the courage to tell you before."

"What else is there?"

Rachelle took a deep breath and looked him in the eyes. "I believe Gabe is cheating on me, with one of his nurses, and I'm not sure what to do."

This one made Daddy angry. "That no good—"

Rachelle raised her palm to silence him. "Wait a minute now, this is the man you and Mom chose for me, remember?"

Her father leaned onto the table and glared at her. "We may have considered him the best match for you as a husband, but that didn't give him free rein to treat you like nothing."

"So you think I should leave him?"

That question cooled his fire. "Take it slow, Rachelle. I'm angry because I'm your father, and I don't want to see anybody hurt you. But I don't know all that goes on in your house. Is he putting his hands on you?"

Rachelle shook her head.

"Alright, as long as he's not hitting you or abusing you in some way, you've got to look inside and figure out whether this marriage is worth saving. He seems like a good man to me, but I don't live in Houston. I see him at his best whenever we're together. You just be assured that whatever issues you have with me and your mother, we love you. We are here for you, and you are never trapped in a situation you can't leave and survive."

Rachelle left her seat and went around the table to hug him.

"Thank you, Daddy."

"You're welcome, baby."

If Jillian and Aunt Irene were right, that God's love was deeper and wider than that of any earthly father's, she was going to be more than okay.

40

Each time she heard the words "Dr. Covington" used in reference to her, Rachelle did a double-take. In her world, that had always been Gabe, heart surgeon extraordinaire.

But since she had begun volunteering at Cynthia's clinic, she too had earned the right to be called by her professional title.

"The state allows me to renew my license every year as a non-practicing optometrist, but I can't officially practice until I obtain sixteen hours of continuing education credits," Rachelle told Cynthia over lunch. She had come to the clinic with Aunt Irene for a few hours today.

Aunt Irene loved reading to the children, and those who were repeat visitors now expected to find her there, waiting with a new book, just for them. Rachelle hadn't been as busy, because not everyone needed eye exams.

When she wasn't assisting with that task, she often sat outside the pediatric exam rooms and watched Cynthia work. Cynthia was masterful at putting her young patients at ease and making the parents feel as if they were doing the most important thing in the world by bringing their children in for regular checkups.

"Do you see this mother?" Cynthia would turn to Rachelle on occasion and say. "Do you see that she brought her son in here for his immunizations so he could start school on time? She values education and health!"

In Rachelle's world, taking children to the doctor for minor aches and pains was as common as seeking help for a high fever or other serious ailment. It was foreign to her that some children would miss the first two weeks of school because their parents hadn't gotten around to taking them to the doctor or to a clinic for routine shots.

Rachelle hadn't considered that making sure babies had enough formula might be secondary to keeping them in Pampers. Cynthia regularly sent new mothers away with a bag of diapers, or a case of formula, and the advice not to stretch it with water every time.

"This is the next best thing to breast milk, and your baby needs all of it to grow," she told them.

Today, over lunch, Cynthia had a To Do list in front of her.

"Since you're going home soon, I want to make sure you keep using your skills," Cynthia said. "I called my friend Vikki in Houston and she's ready to receive you as a volunteer in her pediatric practice until you're fully licensed and ready to move on."

Rachelle's eyes widened. "You did that for me?"

Cynthia waved it off. "We've got to help each other out. And I'm really glad that you're doing something for yourself. You deserve it, and your kids will be proud of you."

But would Gabe? That was the big question. If Veronica's accusations were true and she decided to stay with him, he was probably going to want to continue living life on his terms.

Rachelle reviewed Dr. Vikki Harris's phone number and address. Her practice was located near the rough part of the city, probably with a clientele similar to Cynthia's. Rachelle wanted to help. Gabe would have to get over it.

Rachelle smiled, but inside, she felt butterflies. So much had happened over the past few days. Major stuff. And yet, she felt lighter, like boulders had been lifted from her shoulders.

When she had shared that analogy with Aunt Irene today, on the way to their volunteer session, Aunt Irene had understood.

"That's exactly what is happening, baby," she had said. "You've given your troubles to the Lord. Isn't it amazing?"

Rachelle sat back now and gazed out of the window in Cynthia's small lunchroom. Life was amazing. Even with all of the unanswered questions, mistakes, and missteps, it was worth living fully, like Jillian said.

Before she could take another bite of her sandwich, her cell phone rang. Gabe was calling again. She looked up at Cynthia, hoping her eyes didn't reveal her exasperation. "It's my husband."

Cynthia wiped her mouth with a napkin and stood up so she could get back to work. "Take your time with your call. Your husband is a priority too."

She left and closed the door behind her.

"Too" was the key word.

Rachelle was learning that life and love didn't have to be all or nothing. There were ups and downs, twists and turns, missteps and self-corrections all the time. Even people of faith had setbacks. Aunt Irene would pay a price for her choices, yet she still trusted God to see her through.

Rachelle was learning to keep moving forward, to keep trying to get it right. That's all that Jillian had meant. She didn't know what would happen long term, but she had decided that she needed to fight for this marriage long enough to determine whether there was something there worth saving. She owed that much to God and to her children.

First, though, she wanted to tell Gabe. He might have different plans altogether. When she answered the call, he spoke first.

"Thanks for picking up," he said. "I just wanted to hear your voice. I'm on my way home."

"Really?" Rachelle asked.

"I've made it to London," he said. "We have a layover at Heathrow Airport for a few more hours and I'll be in Houston tomorrow night. I have a lot to apologize for and a lot to tell you about, Rachelle."

He hesitated, and she knew what he wanted to ask—would she be there when he arrived?

Truthfully, she didn't have her feelings all sorted out. She didn't know that she loved him like she should. But like Jillian predicted, the more she learned of God, the more her heart seemed to blossom. She was willing to go home and figure it out.

"I'll be there, Gabe," she said.

"Thank you," he said. "Let me warn you about something though: you won't be coming home to the man you left. I think that's a good thing."

Rachelle appreciated the olive branch. God could make all things new. "I'm a work in progress too, Gabe. I guess we have a lot to talk about."

"And a lot to forgive," he said. "At least I hope you will. I've been wrong and I don't deserve you, but I hope you'll give me a chance to make things better."

Rachelle didn't reply.

"I understand," he said. "I'll be thankful to see you when I get home."

When Rachelle and Aunt Irene left the pediatric office that afternoon, they stopped by a local stationery store. Aunt Irene sat in a motorized cart and shopped for greeting cards.

Rachelle found an aisle filled with journals and perused them until she stumbled upon the perfect one for her Top Ten Things to Do list. The bound book featured a cover illustration of a single yellow rose in a field of dandelions and the phrase, "Give your dreams to God. Who knows where He'll plant them?"

Later that night, when everyone had gone to sleep and she had settled into Reuben's twin bed for the last time, Rachelle pulled out the journal and wrote *Ten Things to Do by the Time I'm 50* in bold, cursive strokes at the top of the first page.

She still didn't have goals for all ten slots, and that was okay. She now realized that for her, discovering what they should be was part of her purpose.

Rachelle did have the first four, however, and she jotted them down in an order that surprised her.

1. Get to know God and become his friend
2. Discover who Rachelle is and love her unconditionally
3. Get to know my husband and fall in love with him
4. Practice optometry three times a week in my own or another thriving practice

That seemed like a full plate, for someone just starting out.

She glanced at her cell phone. It was eight o'clock in San Diego— too late to call her dear friend Jillian, who seemed to be defying the doctor's predictions and holding on to life a few weeks longer. Maybe she would survive longer than any of them believed possible. Rachelle decided to ask Jillian if that was something she should be praying for.

She thought back to a few weeks ago, when she first tried to embrace Jillian's challenge: Be happy. Live fully. Love God.

Now that she was developing a relationship with the Creator, she realized she'd been seeking in the wrong order.

To achieve the goals on her to-do list—in her marriage and in every other facet of her life—she needed to flip the script: Love God. Live fully. Be happy.

Since Gabe was now in a country with regular cell phone capabilities, Rachelle sent him a text.

What do you think about someday supporting an optometry practice?

Minutes later she received a reply:

How do you feel about regular mission trips to Uganda—Dr. Covington?

Her heart did that strange flip-flop that defied description, but equaled hope and excitement. She smiled as she drifted to sleep and thought about the response she sent to her husband.

They had a lot of work to do to repair their marriage, but if he was willing to try, so was she. She was ready to join his and God's team.

THE SOMEDAY LIST
DISCUSSION QUESTIONS

1. Did you understand Rachelle's lingering regret over her long-ago choices?

2. Would having a relationship with God have made accepting these choices any easier?

3. Why was it so hard for Rachelle to craft a list of personal goals?

4. What could she have done to avoid losing herself and still be a good wife and mother?

5. Did Rachelle handle her repeated encounters with Troy appropriately?

6. Did you agree with the advice Rachelle's friends and family gave her regarding her feelings about Gabe? About Troy?

7. Did Gabe's friend, Lyle Stevens, mentor him appropriately?

8. What was most effective in helping Gabe see his flaws and transform? Was his about-face realistic?

9. What purpose did Aunt Irene's character serve?

10. Did you agree with how her issues were resolved?

11. Did Rachelle make the right choice regarding her marriage?

12. Did you agree with how she resolved her issues with Troy?

13. What was the primary thing Rachelle had to give up in order to complete her list?

14. Which character resonated with you most and why?

15. Based on what you've learned from these characters, do you believe second chances are possible?

– COMING JULY 2009 –

Worth a
Thousand Words

Book Two in the
Jubilant Soul Series

1

*I*ndigo Burns rested her elbows on the balcony railing and scanned the crowd that had gathered in the courtyard below to celebrate her achievement and her brief homecoming. "Brief" if that's what one could call the next twelve weeks. In a town the size of Jubilant, three months could feel like twenty, especially after being away for four years and expanding your mind, pursuing your dreams, and falling in love.

Indigo wasn't arrogant— far from it, everyone who knew her well agreed. Instead, she was sure that she had been born to walk a certain path and confident that as long as she had faith, worked hard, and stayed focused, she would succeed.

This afternoon, she leaned to her right and rested her head on Brian's broad shoulder. Without consulting one another, each had come to the party wearing tan linen outfits and brown leather sandals, although his shoes were flat and hers bore two-inch heels.

"This day is perfect," she said, surveying the colorful variety of flowers that bathed the grounds of Jubilant Botanical Gardens. "I feel like God is giving me a thumbs-up and sealing it with a kiss."

Brian tweaked her nose with his thumb and forefinger.

"Then I guess you don't need mine, huh?"

She chuckled and raised her head so his lips could easily reach hers.

Brian delivered the smooch with a smile and she returned the gesture.

"How does it feel to be a college graduate?" he asked. "A summa cum laude one, at that?"

Indigo hugged him sideways. "Feels good, babe. I'm excited about the next chapter."

He wrapped his deep brown arms around her waist and they turned their attention back to her friends and family milling about below, consuming seafood and barbecue, flipping through scrapbooks that contained her photos, and dancing to some of her favorite old school R&B and hip-hop grooves.

At one end of the patio, Brian's parents swayed in sync, tucking their round bodies into each other's like matching puzzle pieces. A few feet away, Indigo's mom and dad sashayed to the riffs of Chaka Khan, a half second off beat as always. And holding center court were Indigo's cousins, Rachelle and Gabe.

Indigo smiled as she watched the tall, lean couple move in close and pull away at the beckoning of the beat. Their eyes remained locked, and at one point, Gabe lowered his head and stole a kiss from his wife.

Indigo blushed and instinctively framed the picture in her mind. If she weren't locked in Brian's embrace right now, she'd grab one of her cameras to capture this miracle. Those two clearly didn't need words to let the family know their marriage was back on track.

The song ended, and before the DJ could start another, Aunt Melba and Shelby climbed the steps to a small stage that had been positioned on the side of the patio. They each grabbed a microphone from its stand and Aunt Melba pointed in Indigo's direction.

"That's where they're hiding," she said into the mic, leading everyone to turn and wave. "Brian, will you please escort the guest of honor to the stage?"

In jest, Brian saluted Aunt Melba. He held out his arm so Indigo could tuck hers inside and they descended the stone stairs. A minute later, Indigo was facing her guests.

Wearing a smile that flaunted her perfect teeth, she stood between her aunt and her best friend and the crowd cheered. The three women looked like purposely posed catalog models of different shades and sizes—Indigo with toffee skin and a thin bone structure that gave her jaw and cheekbones prominent angles; Aunt Melba with her bronze complexion, full red lips, and thick hips; and Shelby, a dark chocolate Hershey's kiss, whose smooth skin and curves made her eligible for Barbie-doll status.

"Aw, ya'll really love me!" Indigo said to the lingering applause. She laughed, but her eyes were glistening.

Shelby pulled out a tissue she had tucked in her palm and passed it to Indigo. "I knew this would happen," she told the other guests. "We haven't said a word about her yet, and she's acting like the Grammy is hers."

Indigo swatted Shelby's arm.

"Seriously though," Shelby said, "It's an honor to be here to celebrate Indigo Irene Burns. For those of you who don't know, I'm Shelby Arrington, Indigo's friend and sister in spirit. We met at Tuskegee University our sophomore year and graduated together yesterday."

Aunt Melba waved. "If any of you don't know me, you better ask somebody!"

The crowd roared.

"I am Indigo's favorite aunt and one of her biggest fans," Melba said. "Indigo graduated with honors yesterday, with a 3.8 GPA. She has received a partial scholarship to the School of Visual Arts in New York City, where she'll move in August to get her master's in photography.

"She's going to tell us what her summer plans are, but her long-term goal is to become as good as, if not better than, famed photographer Ansel Adams," Aunt Melba said.

Shelby continued. "She wants to shoot still-life images for magazines and museums and maybe even for movies. The awesome thing about Indigo is that not only does she *want* to do these things, being the person she is, she'll get them done."

She turned toward Indigo. "Indie, we wish you much success and Godspeed on your journey. And when you hit it big, I'll be your 'Gail.' If Oprah can have a gal pal, you can too!"

Indigo hugged Aunt Melba and Shelby and took Shelby's microphone. The two women stepped aside to give Indigo center stage. She thanked everyone for coming and for supporting her over the years.

"Now, to my parents," Indigo said and shook her head. "I can't say enough. They gave me a camera that used 35mm film when I was ten. Remember those? I took so many pictures that at some point, they began upgrading me to a better model every Christmas.

"They've always believed in me and supported me, even when it meant they had to sacrifice something else. They have taught me, and shown me, that with God and personal grit, there's nothing I can't accomplish. Anything that I've achieved so far, or will achieve, I share those accolades with you, Mama and Daddy. I love you."

Indigo dabbed her eyes with the tissue again and searched the crowd. "Where are Rachelle and Gabe?"

The couple waved from their seats, in the last row of black folding chairs positioned near the stage. Their teenagers, Tate and Taryn, sat next to them.

"Rachelle, you're a first cousin who's more like a big sister, and I appreciate you for that," Indigo said. "Thanks to both of you for giving me this party at this beautiful place. Our usual backyard barbecue was all I had in mind. You're so good to me!"

Gabe stood up and blew her a kiss. "Remember this day when you're rich and famous and I need a loan!" he joked.

Indigo raised an eyebrow and laughed. "Okay, *Doctor* Covington," she said. Just about everyone there knew Gabe was one of the top heart surgeons in the nation and wouldn't need her financial help anytime soon.

"Tell them what you'll be doing this summer," Aunt Melba reminded her.

"I will be interning at the *Jubilant Herald* for nine weeks," Indigo said. "My calling isn't photojournalism, but this will allow me to add a range of photos to my portfolio before I head to grad school. Plus, it will be great to spend the summer at home."

Brian approached Indigo and put an arm around her waist.

"This man isn't on the program," Shelby teased.

Brian winked at her. "Hey, everybody," he said in his husky, laid-back drawl, skipping the self-introduction. "I just want to say that I'm very proud of Indigo. We met at Tuskegee when she was a sophomore and I was a senior." He looked in Shelby's direction. "Our friend over there introduced us, and within half an hour of talking to Miss Indigo, I knew she was special. She hasn't proved me wrong. She has big plans for the future, and I'm praying that I'll be part of them."

Indigo felt tears surfacing again. Brian had never been much of a romantic; this overt show of affection surprised her.

Then he knelt on one knee. She felt faint.

"If you'll take this ring, and agree to become Mrs. Harper, you'll make me the happiest man in the world. Indigo, will you marry me?"

Indigo stared at Brian and tried to process what she'd just heard.

Did he just propose? In front of everyone she knew? Had this man forgotten that he'd be leaving in a few weeks for the Navy's Officer Candidate School, with plans to become a Navy pilot?

Countless emotions engulfed Indigo, from love and gratitude to a tidal wave of fear that churned in the pit of her stomach. As much as she loved Brian, becoming his wife wasn't in her immediate plans. Neither was giving up her first-choice grad school.

"I love you too, Brian," she said weakly, trying to mask her mental wrestling match. How could she say no to this fine, smart brother, who had a bright future ahead of him and happened to be crazy about her?

She couldn't. Especially not in front of all these people.

God forgive me, she prayed silently.

"Yes . . . I'll marry you!" she told Brian.

She flung her arms around his neck and let the tears fall. She did love him, and she did want to be his wife. Just not now—before she, and her dreams, had a chance to blossom.

ACKNOWLEDGMENTS

*M*any people visualize novelists toiling away in isolation as we pound out words about the figments of our imagination. To a certain extent—especially when a deadline looms!—this is true. However, along with carving out the time to write, many of us spend hours conducting research, bringing our characters to life by discussing them with others, and praying for divine creativity and discipline. For me, at least, this is a huge part of the process, and I couldn't accomplish the task without my heavenly Father's guidance or the earthly angels he sends me.

Given that, I first offer a sincere and humble thank-you to God for his unconditional love, grace, and favor: Thank you for granting me the gift of writing and allowing me to serve you as a writer and speaker. I don't take the fact that you've chosen me for granted.

I sincerely appreciate my husband, Donald, and my "little assistants," Syd and Jay, for your love and constant support. Thank you for joining "Team Mommy" and giving me extra time to write so that this manuscript could be birthed.

Heartfelt gratitude is extended to Sharon Shahid, Carol W. Jackson, and Teresa Coleman, my dear friends and first readers, who devoted hours to reading and offering constructive feedback as I created these new characters and plopped them into a fictional setting.

Thank you, as always, to my spiritual mentor, Muriel Miller Branch, for your love, prayers, encouragement, and a sanctuary in which to write whenever I need it. You are an inspiration and a blessing!

Similar thanks is offered to my extended family, especially Dr. Barbara Grayson, Sandra K. Williams, Patsy Scott, Henry Haney, the entire Adams family, Terra Luster, and Lisa Armstead.

I am grateful to everyone who in some way assisted with my research for this book, including Dr. Carolyn Boone, Alexica Lay, Dr. Cheryl Nelson, and John Keltonic, who leads annual mission trips to the Canaan Children's Home in Buziika, Uganda.

Abundant thanks to my agent, Steve Laube; my publicists, Pamela Perry and Barbara Rascoe; and the Revell Books staff for the opportunity to work with you from book idea through publication. A special thank-you is extended to Lonnie Hull DuPont, Brian Peterson, Cat Hoort, Barb Barnes, Twila Bennett, Karen Steele, Nathan Henrion, and Cheryl Van Andel.

I am especially grateful to the many book clubs, booksellers, and media professionals who continue to support my work, and to the following individuals: Bobbie Walker Trussell, Comfort Anderson-Miller, Charmaine Spain, Deborah Lowry, Joe and Gloria Murphy, Gwendolyn Richard, Fritz Kling, Sharon Ewell Foster, Marsha Sumner, Claudia Mair Burney, Marilynn Griffith, Margaret Williams, Vikki Johnson, Carol Mackey, Phyllis Theroux, Rachel Hauck, Joyce E. Davis, Kendra Norman-Bellamy, Tiffany Warren, Victoria Christopher Murray, Jann Malone, Geneva Scott,

Cheryl Miller, Rhonda McKnight Nain, Marina Woods, Sherri Lewis, Adriana Trigiani, Jacquelin Thomas, Virginia DeBerry, Donna Grant, Cindy Windle, Eva Nell Hunter, Rachel Valenti, members of the ACFW Richmond Chapter, the Cannon family, Dr. Linda Beed, Patricia Davis, Beverly Adams, and members of Real Life Ministries and Trinity Baptist Church who have offered their support and encouragement over the years.

And last, but certainly not least, I thank you, the reader, for getting to know these characters and traveling with them to a world not so different from our own. May their journeys inspire your journey.

Here's wishing you abundant grace and new mercies every day.

In His Service,
Stacy

Stacy Hawkins Adams is an award-winning author, journalist, and inspirational speaker. She and her family live in a suburb of Richmond, Virginia. Her other published titles include *Speak to My Heart, Nothing But the Right Thing,* and *Watercolored Pearls.* She welcomes readers to visit her website: www.stacyhawkins adams.com.

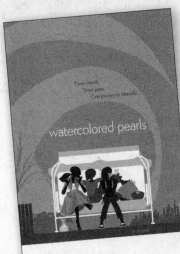